D0341609

the

pearl

diver

NAN A. TALESE

DOUBLEDAY

NEW YORK

LONDON

TORONTO

SYDNEY

AUCKLAND

the

pearl

diver

a novel

JEFF

TALARIGO

PUBLISHED BY NAN A. TALESE
AN IMPRINT OF DOUBLEDAY
a division of Random House, Inc.
DOUBLEDAY is a registered trademark of
Random House, Inc.

Grateful acknowledgment is made to the following for permission
to quote: the Imperial Household Agency, for Empress Sadako's
tanka for Hansen's disease; the Akashi Kaijin Support Group, for the
tanka by Akashi Kaijin, from the poetry collection *Haku Byo,* 1939.

Book design by Terry Karydes

Library of Congress Cataloging-in-Publication Data
Talarigo, Jeff.
The pearl diver : a novel / Jeff Talarigo.— 1st ed.
p.   cm.
1. Pearl divers—Fiction. 2. Women—Japan—Fiction.
3. Leprosy—Patients—Fiction. 4. Leprosy—Hospitals—Fiction.
5. Kokuritsu Ryåyåjo Nagashima Aiseien—Fiction.
6. Japan—Fiction. I. Title.

PS3620.A525P43 2004
813'.6—dc21
2003054893
ISBN 0-385-51051-9

PRINTED IN THE UNITED STATES OF AMERICA

May 2004
First Edition
1   2   3   4   5   6   7   8   9   10

For the 25,000 patients
who lived this story

And for the two Sams in my life,
my grandfather and my son

the

pearl

diver

Settling, white dew

does not discriminate

each drop its home

—Soin

shores

of

isolation

Her words are the only remaining artifact of those days before she arrived.

Nineteen forty-eight. This day, like all of them during the diving season, began slowly. Fixing the strap on her mask, eating a bowl of barley, mending a tear in the hood of her diving suit, eating dried sardine after dried sardine, smoothing a nick taken out of her tub, thinking that the *kanji* letters she had drawn at the bottom of it needed to be repainted. She ate more barley, some dried seaweed, pickled vegetables, drank green tea. The other divers did the same, not much chatter before the dives, concentrating on loading up on carbohydrates for the grueling couple of hours of diving.

Old man Kenichi and the other assistants waited in the boats to take the divers out a quarter of a mile into the Inland Sea. She carried her empty tub, as they all did, before the dive. Only after, when they were sapped of all their energy, did they want, need help. She sat on the edge of the boat, twisting and rolling her ankles, stretching her back and limbs. Some of the women squeezed into flippers, which, not so many years before, they began wearing— they are said to help your speed. That was exactly why she didn't wear them. Maintaining the same pace, the same rhythm, the comfort she found in the more than fifteen centuries of history, the sixty generations of doing things the same way.

In five minutes, they arrived; the boats swayed a bit before finding their balance. She, the youngest of the divers, waited until the others had done so, then tossed her tub and, feetfirst, joined it in the sea. This was the only time each day that her head didn't lead the way. And it was way out there, in the vast waters, that she was never alone. Cedar tubs all around, freckling the water, the divers holding on to the sides until they let out long whistles, released the tubs, shoved them off toward the nine o'clock sun, and disappeared in order of seniority.

The tubs wobbled on the waves, sometimes taking the morning sun from her, then, just as quickly, giving it back. Her arms tight against her sides, her feet swept in slow, steady strokes; waves tossed and jolted her body, the water dimmer, duller, murkier with each foot she went. Sixty feet down, the light was that of an autumn's half-moon. And down there, for the first time, she moved her arms from her sides, doing handstands underwater, feeling for the familiar. Oysters. Sea urchin. Scallops. Lobster. Seaweed. Abalone. Mollusk.

Sometimes, down there at the bottom of the sea, the

hollow cracking of the pick against the rock, the hollow scraping, was sometimes answered very close by. The first time she had heard it, she thought it was an echo, but what she had thought were echoes continued, and when she had turned to her right, there was another diver dislodging an oyster, only an arm's length away.

This day, she chipped and pried at an oyster shell with her metal J-shaped pick, and after only a few chops, it was loose and in her hand. Arching her back, she pushed her feet off the rocks, the same pace as going down, arms at her sides. The water lightened the farther she went; halfway up, the silhouette of her tub appeared. Up, up until she popped out of the water, waist-high, settled back, dropped the oyster into the tub.

Both arms, at the elbows, hooked the tub. She wheezed, gasped, hoarse gasping, her lungs battling each other. The spring winds were strong, the sea clouds had made their way to and dissipated over Honshu. The top of the sea was so much warmer than the bottom. Nothing like a mountain. Sixty feet up, a mountain makes little difference in the temperature. Not the sea. Going down is like autumn into winter. Winter into autumn back up, but the thaw is very slow.

Her lungs cleared, her breathing no longer scratchy, she let out a long whistle, released the tub, gave it a shove off in the direction of the sun, and went back into the sea.

For the final time on that day, a day where she had done more than fifty dives, she headed back up, a lobster in her viselike grip. She surfaced, wheezing; the taut air squeezed out of her lungs to her throat, then through her chattering teeth. She showed Kenichi her lobster—barely able to hold it out of the water—knowing that he was thrilled because, as always, she shared it with him.

But lunch wasn't on her mind. She was so cold that she couldn't even climb into the boat, so tired that she couldn't even drop the lobster into her tub. The cold and exhaustion fed off each other. With his net, Kenichi scooped the catch from her limp, rubbery arm, dropped it into the tub, again stretched out the long fishing net. This time, her empty hands took it; he pulled, lifted her onto the two-step ladder and into the boat.

The sun was almost directly overhead, and although it was well into the eighties, she would not get anywhere near warm for at least a few hours; some days not at all. In the first couple of months of the diving season, she and the other divers balanced on the edge of hypothermia. The boat closed in on the west shore of Shodo Island. Kenichi was jabbering something, the glare of the sun off the sea blinding, buyers gathered on the dock ready to purchase the catch. None of it did she notice, just knew it, for every day was the same. Her glassy gaze was distant, far out there somewhere beyond the blue-on-blue horizon.

Kenichi moored the boat to the cement dock, flung a cigarette stub into the water, helped her out, set her catch next to her, which some of the buyers were already checking over.

"Come on; let's get to the divers' hut before you become stiff enough for me to tie the boat to."

He said that nearly every day and, as if the words were magic, she found herself taking hold of his arm as he led her over to the divers' hut. On the way, she stopped, lowered herself onto the dock, her legs knotted in cramps. She writhed in pain but quickly remembered to try to relax her body. Relax, relax, she told herself, while all the time her body told her to tense, tense. Relax. Leg, neck, back, bottoms of feet. They could strike anywhere. Other divers gave her a quick glance, realizing it was only cramps. She was back on her feet, hobbling to the divers' hut. Again Kenichi reached out for her.

"Can you stand alone?"

"Yes. I'm fine now." She pushed him away, coughed several times, cleared her throat, spat into the water.

He left her there outside the hut, went back to sort everything. She entered, closed the door, and joined the others, her legs still tight as the knots of rope holding the boats to the dock.

Three generations in that hut. Silent as they stripped. Water dripped off the floor, rattling teeth, sucking sounds accompanying the shivers. There was no energy for talk, no need for it. They helped one another with the hard-to-reach places—straps tied in the back of their tops, shedding hoods. She was no longer as self-conscious as she had been in her early months of diving. No longer embarrassed by her chubby but tight body, the gooseflesh, stone nipples, wrinkled hands and feet, tanned face like a mask against her white body, the shaking blue lips.

The unheated freshwater pinged off their bodies, only rinsed the outer skin of the sea from them. The other layers never left. Even in the long months of the off-season, she took the smell of the sea with her to sleep each night. She shivered getting dressed, shivered selling her catch, shivered while shivering.

She had had a good day—three small octopuses, a few dozen oysters, two sea urchins, and some seaweed, half of which she had put aside for her lunch, along with the lobster. The lobster that Kenichi had already removed and was preparing.

Wrapped in blankets, they sat in the divers' hut, drinking hot green or barley tea, cradling cups with hands still wrinkled by the sea, fighting not to think of the cold; in different ways, everyone went about distracting their thoughts from it. Mariko liked to hum old songs, wiggling her toes and fingers as much to warm them as to keep rhythm; Yurika fiddled with her Buddhist prayer beads; Yoko read an Agatha Christie mystery.

But for her, she thought back to that August, not even three years before, when she was certain that the water of the Inland Sea was warmer than it had ever been. Almost hot. She had asked one of the divers if there were any underwater volcanoes in the area. The women had looked up from the sorting of their day's catch, but nobody had laughed or teased like they usually did, her being the youngest of the divers, then barely sixteen. It would be weeks before anyone would dare to laugh, all waiting for the elder diver, Miyako, to show them when it would be okay to do so.

"Why do you ask that?"

She was annoyed that her question had slid out; it was only something that she was thinking.

"Why?" the woman asked again.

"It seems that the water is warmer than I can remember it."

"I've been diving in these waters more than half my life, and I'm old enough to be your mother, and I don't think the water is any different this year than it was before you were born."

She said nothing else.

The next morning, the eighth day of August, the sea was again warmer than normal; she was certain of it, but she kept inside what she thought. That maybe the heat from Hiroshima—less than a hundred miles away—had traveled from its delta, skirted its way through and under the scores of tiny islands of the Inland Sea, warming the waters around Shodo Island. A hot *tsunami*.

And for that week of days, when the water warmed, the divers had worked quietly. Bawdy jokes tucked away for future ears. Going about their business, like the heated Inland Sea went about its: waves rolling in, tide pulling out, rolling in, pulling out, rolling, pulling.

It wasn't until the middle of August that she believed the water had returned to its normal ways. She was in her final few dives when she surfaced and Kenichi told her the diving was finished for the day.

"A few more."

"No more," he said.

There was not a tub, except for hers, out on the water. She'd never been there when a diver died, although she had heard about it happening. Maybe this was what it was like.

Kenichi rowed to shore. Nobody was shucking oysters; they were standing around, a few leaning against the dock, eyes locked onto feet or rocks or just locked. Another bomb, she thought.

"Where did they drop this one?" she asked.

"The war is over," said Miyako, her voice raspy, as if she had smoked a couple of packs of Golden Bats every day of her seventy years, although she didn't smoke at all. She called it "a diver's voice."

"The Emperor spoke. We have surrendered."

"How . . ." she began to ask, but she followed Miyako's eyes to the small speaker hanging on the pole. She looked at the speaker and kept looking at it, as if she could squeeze words from it. Nothing came out. Some of the people around the dock—fishermen, the divers, shoppers— stunned, numb, others with eyes reddened by tears. She didn't know what to do, or say, or whether or not to believe the unbelievable. The Emperor's voice. Couldn't be true, must be true. She continued staring at the speaker for a long while, but nothing came out of it. Not a word.

But on this day, nearly three years later, as the divers slowly warmed up, so, too, did the sounds of lunch. Oyster shells clapped, clinked atop one another on the ground; hot miso soup was slurped, crunchy pickles crunched, one of the divers let out a fart, starting giggles, billowing into waves of laughter, some laughs coupled with still-clattering teeth, making them laugh all the more. She, too, laughed, but she was always aware of her legs, which could be thrown into cramps at any moment.

Lunch, next to the diving, was her favorite time of day.

Her half of the lobster was tasty, boiled in salt water, a little lemon squeezed over the top. She sat the lobster on her barley, alongside the seaweed and several kinds of pickles—radishes, bamboo, cucumbers. Still there was no real talking. A few burps, hiccups, a sneeze, as if that was how they warmed up their voices.

Then a loud scream. Yoko, lucky Yoko, held up a nice large white pearl from inside one of her oysters. It seems as if once a week Yoko finds one, she thought. In her four seasons of diving, she had found nineteen pearls, all at home inside a lacquer box, next to them an eighteen-inch string to measure the length of a future necklace. Yoko must have enough for two necklaces by now, she thought.

And this is how the talking began.

"You seem a little tired today, Chikako."

"Who, me?" Chikako pointed at herself, the chopsticks still in hand, a mouthful of octopus.

"That fine young husband of hers wouldn't let her alone last night."

"My husband?" Chikako laughed.

"I noticed you were walking a little unsteady this morning, even before the dive."

Again Chikako laughed, holding a mouthful of food, which she chewed and swallowed before adding, "I can hold my breath underwater longer than my husband can hold—" She stopped, letting the silence grow, then took another bite of food, never finishing the sentence. The divers were howling. One of them let a piece of octopus dangle from her mouth, keeping the laughter up.

"How about our young diver there?"

All the women turned her way. She squirmed with nervousness. She was still the youngest of the divers. Every spring, she hoped that a new diver, a younger one, would start so she could move out of that position.

"Looks like she's been doing some naughty things, too."

Everyone's eyes were on her forearm, to which Yumi pointed; everyone anticipated Yumi's next words.

"Some sucker bite he gave you."

A few laughs. She looked at the arm, as did everybody. She didn't know what to say, for she had only noticed it a few days before. The reddish spot about the size of a scallop.

"I bumped it on a rock last week," she said.

"That's a sucker bite if I've ever seen one," Yumi added, passing around a pack of sweet red bean cakes. "Only problem is that your lover sure has his direction all wrong. You have to teach him where he's supposed to put that mouth of his. Has to go lower than that."

This brought roars from the others; she, too, couldn't help but laugh. One woman sucked on her arm real loud, adding to the giddiness.

"I hit it during a dive," she repeated, seared with uneasiness, then went on eating, trying to think of something to say that would move the conversation in a different direction. Miyako, the elder diver, rescued her, as she had done many times.

"In twenty years, your body will be a museum of scars," Miyako said, tossing an oyster shell. "You can charge for tours."

She was surrounded by that truth. There wasn't a diver

among them who didn't wear the history of their work on her body. Scarred, thick-bodied women all of them.

She sometimes had to laugh when she thought of her mother and sister, frail and gentle, nothing like a single one of the divers. She dreaded those days when she had to dress up, never feeling comfortable in those sandals, which forced her short, wide feet into a pigeon-toed walk—shuffle, more like it. When her hair was plaited and pulled so tightly into a bun, scrunched together by a lacquer comb, she had a headache the entire day, feeling as if the hair would be uprooted. The sash was so tight, it cut off her breath. But even worse than having to wear the kimono was when she was fitted for a new sash, the woman measuring her; she felt her mother's scouring shame at the thickness, the roughness of her daughter.

But as she sat among the divers, she thought of none of that, only when she made her way home each afternoon did those thoughts creep back into and stay with her until the next morning when she left for the sea.

Miyako talked in a loud voice, although she was sitting no more than five feet from any of them. When Miyako spoke, her tanned, leathery skin glistened. But only on her face, feet, hands—a permanent mask, gloves, socks. Underneath that heavy woolen blanket, Miyako's skin was as white as that pearl Yoko had found. Her more than forty years of diving had brought her lots of money, a beautiful house on the hillside, the gold teeth, respect. She walked away each afternoon, a nice bulge of money tucked between her breasts from her day's catch. Between her mother-of-pearl breasts.

All the divers called Miyako "Grandma" and meant it respectfully. Miyako guided the divers, but it didn't feel as if she were guiding. Like the time when, as a novice, she had asked one of the divers what was the easiest way to loosen an abalone from a rock and Miyako had stepped in and taken her aside.

"We never share secrets of our work or technique. It is okay to be friendly—many of them I love like sisters, daughters—but remember, we are competing against one another. If you don't get that oyster with the giant pearl in it, I will. And I won't be feeling guilty about it. You must develop your own secrets of the trade. Take them to the grave with you."

Miyako, who had rescued her from all the talk about the mark on her arm, now held out some dried kelp. They were all close enough to smell it on her breath, something that she almost constantly chewed when out of the water.

"Want some?" she asked, holding it out. A few took some and Miyako threw an extra piece at Yuki.

"Here, give this to that husband of yours. Good for the hair, thickens and toughens it up."

"He should be eating buckets of the stuff," one diver shouted.

"What's that?" Miyako cupped a hand over her ear, leaned a bit closer.

"I said he should be eating buckets of kelp," the woman said, raising her voice.

"He should be wearing the stuff," another shouted back.

Now, she thought, she could relax a little; the focus had

been wrestled away from her. But she knew that, like the cramps, it could return at any time.

She walked the mile and a half home. Not with the same energy with which she had gone to the sea that morning. Tired, but she was always tired on her trips home, not only from the diving or from having to go up the not so steep hill, but tired because she was going away from the sea. And the next day was Sunday, no diving, making the walk even more arduous.

In her bamboo shoulder basket she carried seven oysters and the small mackerel that Kenichi had given her. She passed limestone boulders; even they weren't the same on the way home. In the mornings, there was a little more color to their paleness. She was warmer, much more so than a few hours earlier, and although the late-afternoon sun was still hot, she, at times, was jolted by a sudden chill, sending a shiver runneling through her body.

Since it was Saturday, she altered her route a little, turning right into the field of olive trees owned by their distant neighbors the Nakamuras. She went to the fifth row and the twelfth tree in it. The same as her birthday—the twelfth day of the fifth month. Without removing the shoulder basket, she dug up the hole, placed a coin with the others inside the small sack, tightened the string, and planted it back into the ground. She evened the soil, patted it down, left the field, whispering a see you next week. Must be nearly five dozen in there now, she thought—one a week each Saturday during the diving season. Saving them for what, she wasn't certain, but for something that would reveal itself in time.

Back on the dirt road, a half a mile from home, the point where the sound of the Inland Sea vanished, but from where she could get a clear view of Honshu, the main island, seven miles away. Sallow pine needle–thin noodles hung drying in the sun. When the sun hit them from behind, they glowed almost like the tiny blue veins against the skin of a baby—thousands and thousands of thin white veins, she thought.

She increased her pace; her father would be finished shortly and she had to help her mother get things ready for dinner. The house was over the knoll. Sometimes she passed her family working in the rice field; sometimes she could get by without them noticing her. If not, she'd have to help out. The best time to sneak by was late in the summer, when the rice rose high enough that she could barely make out her father's hat when he was hunched over in the field.

She cleared the knoll, and her father had his shirtless back to her, the rice nearly at his knees. He stood there smoking, striking his familiar pose, hands behind his back, head up to the sky as if he were gazing at stars. It was the last of the three smoking breaks that he took each day. She walked faster, but as quietly as possible, hoping that he had just begun his break. He had, and she made it all the way to the house without him seeing her. She slid the door open.

"I'm home." She set the basket of oysters and the mackerel at the entrance of the house. Her mother was in the kitchen, preparing miso soup, using the small clams that she had brought home the day before.

"Did you help your father?"

"No, he's about finished."

"What takes you so long getting home?"

"It's Saturday and we have to clean things up."

"We could use the help here, as well."

"I'm busy, too, Mother."

"You dive for a couple of hours. You're not even twenty, too young to be tired."

"It's hard work, Mother. You should try it sometime."

"Why are you always talking so loud? You're right next to me, not way out in the rice field."

"All the divers talk loud. It's a habit."

"Stop the habit when you're in the house. I don't want you acting like those crude people."

"They're not crude. We work around fishermen all day and we talk loud because of all the noise of the sea. I tell you this nearly every day, Mother."

"You're shouting again."

"Maybe the diving is damaging my ears, like all the other divers."

"And you're getting to be like all of them. The body and toughness of a man. We're working on finding your sister a husband, and you're going to be next. What kind of man wants a woman who's tough and loud-talking?"

"I brought home some oysters and a mackerel. Should I go and clean them up for dinner?"

"Yes. We'll be eating early; it's Saturday."

She went to the front, slid the door shut, saw that her father had finished his final break of the day and was, once again, over the rows of rice. She opened the basket, imagining that she was deep in the sea, the pick in hand, chipping at one of the oysters. That thought didn't stay with her for long because she knew that very soon her father would be home and she would be serving him tea and dinner and *sake,* and the next day was Sunday, the longest day of the week, a day without the sea.

The exact moment. Her eleventh dive, August 27, 1948, wedged upside down between two boulders. A calm sea. Struggling with a large abalone, which had its suction cups pasted to a rock. Not thinking about time, but always aware of it. Nearing her limit in her lungs, that rush of excitement on the edge of pain, fear. Daring herself not to let go, for if she did, she knew from hard lessons learned that the abalone would escape between the rocks and she'd never get it. Pulling, prying, using the bar as a wedge. Pulling when she lost her grip on the mother-of-pearl shell and cracked her left forearm off a rock, nearly causing her to breathe a deadly breath. The abalone slithered deeper between the rocks, forever away from her.

Working her way back up, keeping her pace, no matter how much her lungs screamed, urged her to hurry. Knowing that she was bleeding, those rocks, volcaniclike rocks, sharp as razors, but strangely she didn't feel anything. She surfaced, empty-handed. She took hold of her tub with her right arm, dragged it along the water to the boat. Trailing her, a red blood line. She saw it but didn't even feel the warmth of the blood.

"Looks like you got yourself a nice cut," said Kenichi.

"It's okay. Doesn't even hurt."

Kenichi gave her one of those faces that said he didn't believe a word of it. But it didn't hurt. Looked bad, though. A deep but clean gash in the center of the red spot that she had first noticed a couple of months before. The spot one of the divers had called a "lover's bite." But as she was helped into the motorboat, she thought it must be adrenaline.

Thirteen oysters, three sea urchins. It was only the second time that she had come back early. The first, the day of the surrender.

Only a few more weeks left in the diving season, she thought, watching the foamy tail left behind by the motorboat. Kenichi had bought the boat that spring. She liked the rowboat much better. She wanted to cover her face now against the smell of the burning oil, but she was holding the towel against her arm, red seeping into it. She anticipated, waited for the pain to match the ugliness of the wound. Knew that it should hurt, knew this from past falls, past pains. And even before reaching the shore, she was readying her mind for the next day, when she would have to dive through the pain.

But the pain never came. Traces of it near her wrist and up by the bicep, still that mysterious numbness on her forearm. She skipped the next two days of diving, fearing an infection, went to the sea on her bicycle, her older sister's really, but she had awakened before her and taken it. Trouble when she returned home, but at that moment, the breeze from the sea off her face, through her short hair, grazing her underarms, the future, or the past, wasn't in her thoughts.

When she arrived, she felt left out, not because they weren't talking and laughing with her, but because they were all getting ready and the days of the diving season were few. Autumn was near; she could feel it in the air that morning. For her, the most difficult time was the first couple of weeks after diving season. No sea. Only out in the fields with her family, harvesting rice. Then winter. The sea too cold for even a visit. Six agonizing months. She hated winter—but despised autumn, for it preceded it, and she felt the harshness of December long before it ever got to her.

　　　　　　*　　　　*　　　　*

A lingering wasp from the remnants of summer. Her only company in that abandoned warehouse. Still some time before the knock at the door and the food was left outside. Sometimes a little note, sometimes only the thought of one; several times there had been a newspaper.

At first, she wasn't sure whom she was hiding from— her family, the doctor, herself? Then, sometime in her first week there, she received a note from Miyako telling her that the police had been to see her. In those early days of hiding, she used to peek through the crack between the metal doors, watching, listening. Sometimes for hours. And when she would see Miyako coming, she'd place her palms against the door, waiting for the knock, and she would keep them there, clinging to the very last pulse that it left behind. Miyako would set the food on the ground, scurry off, not too fast so as to call attention to herself, not once glancing back at the warehouse, although she had imagined, knowing her, that it tortured Miyako not to do so.

Miyako began leaving the food in paper bags, not in a plastic lunch box like she had that first day. She was again at the door, peeking through the crack, when Miyako returned the second day. She stared in disbelief at the fear on the face of the strongest woman she knew, disbelief as she saw her go find a metal pipe and then use it to push the empty plastic lunch box away, pushing and pushing until she could no longer see her through the crack in the door. It was the only time that she allowed herself to cry, to feel some self-pity. After that, when she had finished eating, she rolled up the paper bags and tossed them into the corner of the warehouse.

Dear, sweet Miyako. She knew the day the doctor told her the news that if there was anyone she could tell, it was Miyako.

More than a month had passed since she had cut her arm; diving season had finished, a week into October. Then, the second spot on her lower back—that one, too, had no feeling. And the constant stuffy nose. She left her family to the rice harvesting and went the three miles into town to the doctor's.

She had heard about the disease, how you should stay away from those people, how they were a burden to the country during the war. Filthy. Cursed. Should she fear herself? No, only that she had to tell her family. That, she didn't even let herself think of, didn't stop thinking of it.

She didn't know where to go. Her family still had most of that afternoon left in the fields. She had promised to be home to help. But what were promises at that time?

She walked away from town, feeling as if everyone she passed knew about her. But how could they? None of her spots were visible under her thin cotton jacket. A girl passing through town. How soon before everyone knew? Before the doctor told one person, and then it would spread like the fine red sand that blew in from China every winter? Covering everything.

She had never been to Miyako's house, had only been as far as she was that afternoon, up by the thicket of bamboo along the path leading to it. That was where she waited, trying to allow the sunlight, weaving its way through the bamboo, to distract her from her thoughts, the flecks of dust floating, the illuminated insects flittering through the beams. Tried.

Although the diving season was over, Miyako still went to the sea during autumn, where she passed a few hours each day. Only a week had passed, she thought. The following diving season twenty-nine weeks, two hundred and three days, to go. Or more. That thought was too much. She tried going back to the midafternoon sun and the bamboo.

She saw Miyako approach around the bend, about fifty yards down the path. Walking deliberately, strong, short steps—a half waddle. When Miyako was about ten yards away, she stepped out in front of her.

Neither of them took a step closer. Did she already know? Impossible. But maybe not so impossible. The look on

Miyako's face told her that she knew, but maybe it was her own look that told Miyako something was terribly wrong.

"What brings you up here?" Miyako asked. Still, neither had made the next step, forward or back, locked in the moment like at the bottom of the sea, all time stopped.

"I'm sick." The words choked and garbled.

"Sick?"

"Remember when I cut my arm a couple of months ago?"

Miyako didn't speak, only nodded.

"I'm sick," she said again.

Miyako took a step toward her, then another.

"Leprosy."

Miyako didn't move, her next step severed by the word.

"From that cut?"

"No, the spot was there before I cut my arm. Last week, I found another—on my back."

Miyako appeared as though she wanted to retrace those two steps she had just taken, but her stubbornness wouldn't allow it.

"What are you going to do?"

"The doctor says I have to go to a sanatorium."

"When?"

"I have to talk to my family first. Soon. The doctor told me that I can never dive again because I could spread the disease through the water to the other divers, to the children who play there in summer."

Neither moved nor talked. A distant ship wailed its horn. She took a couple of steps toward Miyako, bowed deeply to her, and walked away, looking back only once when she reached the bend, and Miyako was still standing where she was when she had left her.

Back in the warehouse, a couple months' worth of paper bags pyramided in the corner, she waited for Miyako's knock on the door. She thought of her family and how it had been six weeks since harvest. How she had never returned, only left Miyako's, and, after wandering aimlessly for hours, how she had ended up in the warehouse. How she had opened the door, closed it, fell asleep, woke up, felt hungry, wrote a note and then placed it on Miyako's door, and the next day there was a knock and the lunch box sitting outside.

And that was how it had been every day, and for how many more, she couldn't even imagine. She knew only that she was standing up because she had heard the knock; it was time to get her lunch and allow the five seconds of sunlight, which the open door provided, to flood into the warehouse.

Without peeking through the crack, she opened the door. There was no paper bag out there, only two policemen. She stepped into the afternoon—the cloudy skies lashed at her eyes—closed the door behind her, knowing that the dim bar of sunlight that had snuck into the warehouse had already been strangled.

The policemen led her away, keeping a distance. She turned and wondered about that day's lunch, and when it arrived, how long would it sit outside before the rats got to it, how long before Miyako stopped leaving the food?

She faces the back of the man digging the oars into the water, watching him bury her past in the heavy mist of the Inland Sea. His rowing is fluid but tense. Icy waves slap at them. Today, she wishes for Kenichi's motorboat. If the man didn't know where they are going and what is awaiting them on the other shore, they would probably be facing each other right now, perhaps even speaking. If he didn't know where they are going and what is awaiting them, maybe he would even glance at her once in awhile. A normal-looking nineteen-year-old girl.

She opens the cloth in which the lunch has been wrapped. Cold, hard rice. The rice balls simple, covered in dried seaweed. If this were a normal day, she would consider herself lucky. Rice. A rare treat all through the war and even now, three years after. She eats two of them. No enjoyment at all, only to fill her up. She asks the man if he would like some. She sees his shoulders tighten, perhaps two strokes with the oars a little out of rhythm. Quickly, he recovers. His silence colder than the rice or the wood of the boat or her ears.

Looking over the side, she tries imagining the depth of the water, but she can't concentrate. She leans back and holds her breath, counting the strokes. Fifteen. Twenty. Forty. She could continue keeping the breath within her, but she stops, noticing that the mist has thinned out and that Nagashima is close. Close enough to tell that the trees are pines and not cedars. If the water wasn't so rough, she's sure she could see the bottom of the sea. Jump right off and touch it. Her place.

He breaks his rhythm, rowing faster now, maintaining that pace until they hit the rocky bottom, throwing her against the side of the boat.

He never even steps off the boat, but for the first time on this long day, he faces her. She, on the cement dock; he, working the oars once again. Always with his back to the place he is going, facing the place he is leaving. She watches him edge away. He must be exhausted, but, wanting so desperately to get away from this place, he rows and rows. But he isn't that far away, perhaps fifty yards, when he does stop. The boat wobbles, shifts under his weight as he removes the left oar from its latch; he picks it up, as far away from the blade as is possible. He leans over and, using the blade of the oar as a shovel, scoops and flings into the water the two rice balls she left behind for him. They disappear like stones. He replaces the oar and begins digging, his back to her past.

As our generals hang in the December wind, the time line of her isolation begins. It is the future Emperor's fifteenth birthday, forty-one years before he will begin his reign.

She stands here on this dock—the receiving dock—watching the man row until he, like the rice balls, fades into the sea. The sea. From this day on, it will forever be different for her. Not hatred—she will never hate it—only something that separates. It had always been something that she thought connected—island to island, fishermen to home. But today it is, and always will be, a separator.

Two men, wearing doctor's masks, lead her along the narrow dock, past several rowboats much like the one she arrived on. They pass a small shack, many kinds of farm equipment under its tin roof. She feels sick to her stomach, the cold rice like lead. She stops, catches her stomach from leaving her.

"Hurry up, there's much to be done," one of the men says, a few steps ahead.

A couple of deep breaths help a little and she follows the men into a large building, splotches of ivy clinging on the outside walls. A wooden shoe box is off to her right. The ceiling is higher than any she has ever seen before. She removes her shoes, and as she is about to place them in the box, a woman wearing thick rubber gloves comes out of nowhere, rips them from her hands, and drops them into a burlap sack.

"Into that room and place all your belongings in one of those bags." Still, the men are several steps away from her. Never closer.

Dirty curtains, covering the glass on the door, are lifted by the wind brought in through the entrance. She steps inside, and before she can even close the door, her stomach is lost all over the floor. The smell of chemicals staggers her. The room is large, made even larger by the ceiling. A nurse hands her a bucket and a rag.

"Close that door and clean this up. When you've finished, go over there behind the curtain and remove everything."

She throws up again. The nurse's rubber boots flop as she hurries away.

She cleans up, a stain left behind on the floor, then goes over and opens the curtain. A woman, old enough to be her mother, sits naked on a dirty mattress. Her left hand in front of her pubis, her right can cover only half of her breasts.

"Excuse me. I'm sorry."

She walks out of the curtain-partitioned room.

"Hurry up and get undressed." The nurse points her back to where she has just left.

The older woman turns her back to her, the long, bent fingers still where they were when she first entered. Red spots on her back. Some larger the farther down one looks. Her hair is like a swallow's nest after a typhoon, strewn all over, eggs long gone. Her face, round as a ramen bowl, is untouched except for one red spot under her right eye. She moves as far away from the woman on the bed as she can, turns her back, undresses. She hides her change purse inside the pocket of her jacket. The room is cold; many times she has been colder—those early-May dives—but the shame she feels gives this cold a raw edge to it.

The curtain snaps open. She stands, for the first time in her life, naked before a man. Like those of the woman on the edge of the bed, her hands, too, instinctively cover the most private parts of her being.

"Move your arms and stand up straight," the doctor orders. She hears the words, but his mouth and nose are covered by a white mask, making it difficult to follow what he says.

"Stand up straight!" She sees his mask move up and down, again hears the words, sees the doctor's eyes behind black-rimmed glasses that sit crooked on his nose. He steps toward her. She uses the side of the bed as a support but feels her knees weaken, and with her arms still covering her, she hits the floor. The ceiling is a clear blue sky. Endless. The older woman speaks words she doesn't understand; her hideous claws touch her face.

"Don't touch me!" she screams. "Nobody touch me!"

The older woman jumps away, her hands back to her body.

"Get up so we can disinfect you," yells the doctor.

She reaches for her clothes, but they are gone; stabs at a bedsheet, but there is only a mattress. She starts to cry.

"Stop this foolishness."

The doctor clenches her arm, jerks her up by it. He has her above the elbow, the thick rubber glove a slimy cold, like a raw oyster in January. She's taken into another room. The doctor tells her to lie on the bed, a plastic sheet atop it. First on her stomach. He checks behind her ears, the nape of her neck, under her arms, down her back, all the time making these sounds like he is sucking his teeth. He spreads her legs; the glove hurts as he touches her down there, makes all her skin ache, as if she's sliding naked on ice. She notices, on her left arm, a large bruise already beginning to spread from where she fell on the floor. Spreading over the diving scar within the spot. Years ago. She keeps her eyes on the spot, the blue-green-black bruise scattered inside, around it. Keeps her eyes on it, tries to create a map from it. Yakushima. Like the island of Yakushima, round except for a little deviation on the top left side. His hands down the backs of her legs, the soles of her feet.

"Turn over."

She does, knowing nothing that she is doing. Chilled tears dribble, drip down the side of her face, plunk against the plastic bedsheet.

His hands over her breasts, against her stomach, inside her, down her thighs, across her diving-scarred knees, her feet, between her toes.

"Get up," he says, leaving the room.

The worst is over. You have been through the worst. She keeps telling herself this.

A nurse comes in and leads her to the back of the building. Colder than she has ever been. A startling smell of chemicals.

"Keep your eyes closed."

She is covered, drenched, in the chemical odor. A second layer of skin. She inhales, trying to strangle tears that want out. Her throat burns, her nose drips, and her eyes release, this time, boiling tears. Her skin scoured all over, but still the cold rubber glove between her legs. She is led out of the room, given a thin robe, and is standing before a young man at a desk. Sweating. Shivering. Her upper left arm hurts where the doctor grabbed her, the red spot on her forearm without feeling, the bruise spreading.

"I have a few questions for you, but these are only for our records. Your life begins here right now, at this very moment. Do you understand that?"

"Yes," she answers.

"How old are you?"

"Nineteen."

"Where are you from?"

"Shodo Island."

"Okay. Your number is two six four five. Don't forget it. Two six four five. Repeat it."

"What about taking down my name?"

"I told you to forget everything. Name and all. Wipe it out of your head as if it were never there. Same for your family. Everything for you begins here today, right now. Your number, what's your number?"

"Two six four five."

"Again."

"Two six four five."

"Now you must choose a new name."

"But I have a name."

"Didn't you listen to what I told you? You have caused great shame to your family, and for their sake, have your name struck from the family register. As if . . ." He pauses.

"As if I were dead."

His eyes don't like what she said.

"Today is the beginning of your past. December the

twenty-third, 1948. You are born today. It will be easier on you if you think of it this way."

"But I haven't thought of a new name."

"You have until tomorrow."

The groaning of the rowboats tied to the wooden dock outside. Thinks that is what she hears. She stares up at the ceiling. She is tired, more tired than the man who has rowed her here. Even he must be home asleep by now.

All around her, on this first night of her isolation, bodies. Some are already spotted like that of the older woman earlier in the day. Others worse than that. Some with faces, limbs already contorted. Several are like her—no visible sign until they are naked. She doesn't use the blanket, not sure who wrapped themselves in it the night before. She curls up within herself, but it is cold. Not as cold as the doctor's gloves. Never that cold again. She covers her face with her hands to block out some of the disinfectant's stench, but her hands stink of it, everybody does, this room does, this building, this island. For the first time in years, she doesn't smell the sea on her skin.

She tries thinking of a name. It doesn't sound all that difficult to do. Pick a name. When she was little, she often had make-believe names when playing. It was easy. She never thought of it before now, but we are lucky, for the burden of choosing a name is put on the parents, not us. But now she is both the parent and the newborn. And not only a first name, a family name, as well.

The woman next to her can't sleep, either; she's been

moving around all night. She asks the woman's name. The woman mumbles something that she doesn't understand. Maybe she is asleep, she thinks. She asks again. Again, she doesn't understand. A man, a couple of mats away, speaks.

"Mang. Her name is Mang. She doesn't speak much Japanese."

"Doesn't speak Japanese?"

"She's Korean."

She doesn't know what to say. What's a Korean doing here? The man breaks the silence.

"My name is Shikagawa. Why do you want to know everybody's name?"

"Because they said I must choose one."

"That's not easy. You have to think of something happy in your life. Make a name from that."

"We're not supposed to think of our past."

"That's only what they say. They know that's impossible, but what else are they to tell us?"

"Why did you choose Shikagawa?"

"When I was a child, I used to see a deer drinking from the river near my family's home. So I chose Shikagawa— deer drinking from the river."

"That's beautiful."

"At least something I have is. That's why it's so important for you to give this some real thought. I will be quiet now. Good night. I'll ask you your name in the morning."

There is a single dream that she has in this first week. Maybe she has so few dreams because she sleeps so little. It is the same dream over and over, very short but exactly as the previous one. The man who rowed her here has arrived back at Shodo Island and he has dragged his boat ashore. And although it is late December, he removes the fingerless gloves from his hands, then his hat, jacket, shirts, socks, pants, underwear, and throws them all in the boat. He empties a container of kerosene over it, tosses a match. Everything is in black and white. Even the flames. The man doesn't stand there to get warmed by the fire, but runs away naked, and she is here on this shore, watching him through the flames until she sees him no more.

the

artifacts

of

nagashima

Every artifact has a dozen stories—a thousand.

ARTIFACT Number 0012
The money of Nagashima

The Coins:

> *One Sen:* oval-shaped. The front: black, trimmed in gold, a hole in the middle, the amount, along with the *kanji* for Nagashima Leprosarium. The back: plain bronze, no design.
>
> *Five Sen:* round-shaped. The front: black, trimmed in gold, a hole in the middle, the amount, along with the *kanji* for Nagashima Leprosarium. The back: plain bronze, no design.
>
> *Ten Sen:* round-shaped, a little larger than the five-sen coin. The front: black, trimmed in gold, a square hole in the middle, the amount, along with the *kanji* for Nagashima Leprosarium. The back: plain bronze, no design.

Fifty Sen: round-shaped, a little larger than the ten-sen coin. The front: black, trimmed in gold, no hole in the middle, the amount, along with the *kanji* for Nagashima Leprosarium. The back: plain bronze, no design.

One Hundred Sen: oval-shaped, the largest of all the coins. The front: gold, trimmed in black, no hole in the middle, the amount, along with the *kanji* for Nagashima Leprosarium, a handheld fan design on the bottom. The back: plain gold, no design.

The Paper Money:

One Yen: rectangular-shaped. The front: plain white, with black ink. The date handwritten down the left side, the *kanji* for Nagashima Leprosarium printed from right to left across the bottom, the amount in the middle. The back: plain white.

Five Yen: rectangular-shaped, a little larger than the one-yen bill. The front: plain white, with black ink. The date handwritten down the left side, the *kanji* for Nagashima Leprosarium printed from right to left across the bottom, the amount in the middle, to the right side of which is a drawing of a small sunrise over an island, the thin beams of the sun stretching far; to the left side of the amount, a picture of pampas grass bending in the wind. The back: plain white.

And on the seventh day of the first week, the final week of 1948, she, like all of the new patients, receives her money.

ARTIFACT Number 0022
Those who arrived in 1948

a third-year university engineering student
four fishermen
two mothers
a boy who just completed seventh grade
a tanka poet
three World War II veterans and a
      twenty-year-old kamikaze who lived
a young woman two weeks from her marriage
a mah-jongg gambler
five high school girls and boys
a twenty-six-year-old man who worked in the ship-
      yards
a semiprofessional baseball player
three schoolteachers—two women and a
      man who was a high school band director
a Buddhist priest
three Christians
a fish market auctioneer
two government office workers and a policeman
five Koreans—a woman and four men
a sushi shop owner
two members of the Communist party
two coal miners
a train conductor
three nurses
seven farmers
two construction workers

one law student
and a pearl diver

ARTIFACT Number 0196
A rusty farm sickle

She sees the man with the sickle in his right hand, but she sees the same thing many times each day. The patients, who are healthy enough, do everything here: gardening, fishing, nursing, teaching, constructing buildings. They are both patient and staff. So, yes, she sees him, but he doesn't strike her as doing anything unusual or suspicious. Just walking by with a small sickle in his hand. Many people carrying or pushing all kinds of things: sickles, rakes, shovels, hand plows, wheelbarrows.

He is not much older than she, maybe twenty-five, no more than thirty. She does know that he's a newer patient and that, like her, he has almost no physical signs of his disease. He goes around without a shirt, not a mark on his torso, only the large red spot on his left hand. A spot that stands out even more because of how suntanned he is.

She is up on the hill in Building A-15, giving Mr. Mimura's legs a massage, when she hears screaming down near the sea, where most of the gardening is done. She goes to the window, doesn't see anything, but continues to hear the commotion.

"I'll be right back, Mr. Mimura."

"Take me with you."

"I'll only be a minute. I want to see what the screaming is about, that's all."

"Take me."

She picks Mr. Mimura up from the bed—he's like a bony bird, weighing not much more than her cedar tub filled with a day's catch—places him in a wheelbarrow. Mr. Mimura's been here since 1933, fifteen years before she arrived. He is in his mid-fifties, one of the oldest patients. She takes him outside and sees a large group of people running up the hill, carrying someone. She hurries toward them, nearly spilling Mr. Mimura out of the wheelbarrow. They rush on past and she follows them to the hospital. The man is bleeding profusely from his left arm, but it is all the mud mixed with the blood that keeps her attention. A muddy, bloody trail all the way up the path leading from the sea.

It isn't even fifteen minutes before the doctor comes out and says that the man has died, lost too much blood. The doctor tells several patients to carry the body over to the crematorium and dispose of it.

She pushes Mr. Mimura back to the shed, but his gnarled hand punches at her arm.

"Go down to the beach."

"Not today, Mr. Mimura. I have many things to do."

"Down to the gardens. Now."

Mr. Mimura is always polite and calm, and the only reason that she takes him down to the gardens is because his demanding tone is so out of character. It's only up a little hill and down another, and it isn't that hot, the end of April. There are a few people working in the gardens, and Mr. Mimura points for her to go off to the right, to the gardens closest to the beach.

"Help me out of here."

She lifts him out of the wheelbarrow, helps him on those bird-thin legs over to where the potatoes are planted. Beside a large rock is a bloody sickle—like the sickle she saw the man with this morning—dried maroon by the sun. On the rock is the man's left hand, the large red spot still on the back of it. She stares at the mountain that sits at the far end of the peninsula.

"Help me back to the wheelbarrow."

She supports Mr. Mimura, lifts and sits him in the wheelbarrow, pushes him all the way up the hill, back down the other, past the shed and all the way around the small inlet to the other side of Nagashima.

They still haven't begun to cremate the man. Mr. Mimura, with her help, walks over to the naked body. She looks. Several scars on his right shoulder, scars whose history none of them in this room will ever know. She turns her head away, but when Mr. Mimura places the severed left hand on top of the man's chest, she looks again, and they all stand there waiting for his body to be slid into the furnace.

ARTIFACT Number 0151

> A photo of Health Minister Tsujino and
> the thirteen heads of the nation's leprosaria
> Tokyo, Japan, June 25, 1949

Sitting around the oval-shaped table, a thicket of suits. Clockwise: Dr. Nishi, Dr. Yoshimura, Dr. Etoh, Dr. Barayama, Dr. Nomura, Dr. Ishihashi, Dr. Oishi, Dr. Nakamori, Dr. Saitoh, Dr. Wakabayashi, Dr. Yamashita,

Dr. Fujita, Dr. Ikuta. At the head of the table, Dr. Tsujino, director of the Ministry of Health.

Cigarette smoke already pushed to the ceiling settles back down near their heads. Health Minister Tsujino has to squint through the fog in order to see the other thirteen men in the room. He gives a deep bow toward the top of the table before speaking, nearly touching his teacup with his head.

"With the development of the Promin drug, and its very positive results in stopping the progression of the disease, we can now cope with the future. We must begin thinking about releasing some of the patients. At least the ones who have recently been admitted."

A hush hovers. Minister Tsujino waits, takes a couple of sips from his now-tepid green tea, then waits some more before giving another bow and speaking again.

"This drug is what we have been searching for—for a long time. A chance to get rid of this disease. Conditions now are considerably different from what they were forty years ago, when we had to quarantine the patients. Considerably different from even a year ago. It may be time to change the Leprosy Prevention Law. Each one of you should begin immediately compiling a list of your most recent patients, starting with those admitted since the beginning of 1946, and also those who have only mild cases of the disease. With them, at least many of the physical scars aren't so noticeable. They should be able to be reintroduced into society. If not their own communities, then at least some other place."

Again, when he stops talking, there is nothing but silence. It is shattered this time, shortly after he stops.

"We can't subject the citizens of this nation to these people. Imagine the panic that would spread. It would be a calamity," says Dr. Nishi.

"But if we release only those whose disease hasn't progressed, treat them with the drug as outpatients. Other countries have started implementing this policy. We have nearly seventeen thousand patients in our facilities. If we can release even forty, fifty percent of them in the near future, think of all the money that could be saved. Some of the smaller facilities could even be shut down; the remaining patients at those facilities could be transferred to the larger ones. Up here. Down in Nagashima, Kagoshima, Kumamoto."

"You're not thinking of the greater good of the people. Our own Dr. Mitsuda's theory, back in 1931, clearly states that these people should be isolated from society. States that clearly. His theory is internationally known."

"All due respect to Dr. Mitsuda, whom I have known for many years now, back to the days when he was director at Nagashima, and I have much admiration for him, but his theory of isolating patients was before the introduction of Promin. This drug changes that. The theory, as correct as it was at the time, ceases to apply today."

"We have been using this drug for less than two years. We can't go releasing them into society. Have you seen some of these people? They would be ridiculed for the rest of their lives. And what about them going and getting married and having children?"

"Yes, of course I've seen them, Dr. Nishi. That's why we should slowly release them. The best patients first. Some of them have almost no physical signs of the disease. As for them starting families, we have the Eugenics Law enacted last year; that can deal with the problem before we release them."

"Whom do they go to? Their families have disowned them. Their names have essentially been eliminated from the registers. They've had no contact with society."

"But if we have the disease stopped and it doesn't get any worse, maybe their families will reconsider. I'm talking about the lowest-risk patients. Treated as outpatients. Besides, it is our duty to educate the public."

The quiet crashes back into the room; the electric fans blow it around, dispersing it all over and back again.

"What do the others in this room think about this?" asks Minister Tsujino.

There is no response; the rotating of the fans click, click. A few of the men pat the gathering sweat on their faces, let out stifled sighs, pat the backs of their necks, sweat impeding their white collars.

"How about a show of hands for all of those in favor of releasing patients back into the public?"

Although, because of the smoke, it is difficult to see the people farthest from him, Minister Tsujino knows he doesn't have to see, for not a hand is lifted from the wood of the oval table.

ARTIFACT Numbers 0147 and 0272
A red stone with a black swath running
through it; a worn one-yen coin.

From the rocks at the bottom of the cliff, she stares at the bleeding wound of the morning horizon. The tide backtracks, leaving only small puddles in the crevices of the rocks she sits on.

She knows of twenty-three patients who struck these rocks, their final breaths taken on them. What was the last thing that they saw? Was it something of beauty? Like the white heron she sees pinkened by sunrise, perched one-legged, checking from the corner of its eye a fish leaping a foot out of the water. Or did they close their eyes, nothing left for them to see? Was it on a moonless night, sneaking away from their room, feeling their way up the dirt path, past the bamboo, and finally that thin, crooked cedar that stands atop the cliff, on a moonless night when nothing could be seen, eyes open or not? How many more—than the twenty-three that she knows of—in those seventeen years before she arrived?

She helped to remove many of them from these rocks. Helped carry their bodies along the rough shore, over to the area past the farmers of Nagashima, who removed their hats, rested their hoes and rakes, past the fishermen of Nagashima, the nets bunched at their feet. The bodies were angled into a wheelbarrow and were taken on their final journey to the crematorium.

This morning, she is not here to take away any bodies, only here because she likes the place. This place of death makes her feel so strangely alive. A place to get away, to be alone, and that is very difficult on this island, for her, and even more so for the patients who are wheelchair-bound, blind.

Tucked among the shallow gorges of the rocks, she sees the west coast of Shodo Island, where, a little bit around the corner, in a few short hours, the divers will begin diving. Sometimes, but not as often now, she imagines that she can feel the energy from the divers cutting through the seven miles of the Inland Sea. Like that hot *tsunami* coming from Hiroshima that she felt in August— the August in this country that will never need a year to accompany it.

The sun has trudged its way atop the hill at the eastern edge of the island; a fishing trawler heads home while the large temple bell of Nagashima gongs out the hour. Slow. Slow. Slow. Slow. Slow. Slow.

Several early mornings this week, the rocks have bared, then sunned themselves, building a path to a tiny island across from Nagashima. A large cement *torii* gate stands at the front. Ever since arriving here, she has thought of crossing the one hundred yards to the island. She has stopped, each time wondering if it would be considered an attempt at escape. How could it be? The island is surrounded by the Inland Sea, no land, other than Nagashima, within a mile of it. But the rules are not hers to make or break.

Then, the week before, she saw a man cross over to the island and knew that she, too, must cross.

The sea recedes, leaving less than a yard from her to the rocks that have begun making the path to the island. Before going back to begin her day, a beautiful red rock at the bottom of the suicide cliff catches her eye. She picks it up. Almost like coral, she thinks, bits of white shells fossilized in it, a glossy black swath sweeping over the stone, as if someone has swooped, only once, a calligraphy brush along it. She carries the stone back up the slight grade leading away from the sea.

While giving Miss Min a massage, she asks about the island. Miss Min arrived here in 1943, when she was brought over from her homeland as a war slave along with her brother to work in the Kyushu coal mines. At the port, she was discovered to have leprosy and wasn't sent to the mines, but here. Although less than ten years separate the two of them, Miss Min's disease is much further along. While giving massages, she tries not to get involved too emotionally with the patients, tries not to think too much, but with Miss Min, it is most difficult. Sitting before her is not a woman in her early thirties, but twenty years older than that. Hardly a shadow of what she must have been less than ten years ago remains.

She likes Miss Min, who, almost always while she is giving her a massage, tells stories—real or not, she isn't sure. Sometimes she listens intently to the stories; at others, she allows the words to meld into the rhythm of her kneading hands.

"Have you ever crossed over to that small island?" she asks Miss Min.

"Why would I want to?"

"To see what's over there."

"I'm sure somebody's been there. There's that giant *torii* gate."

"Let's go sometime."

"Are we allowed?"

"I don't see why not. Not much of a place to escape, is it?"

"Not much of a place."

Two days later, they wait together at the dock, watching the water peel itself from the stones.

"We have only about an hour and a half before the sea comes back."

She takes Miss Min's hand, the fingers having collapsed to half their size. The hand is ice-cold, although the autumn air hasn't yet shaken all of summer from its breath.

"What are you afraid of?"

"I told you I can't swim."

"Who needs to swim. You can walk, can't you?"

"What if the tide comes in early?"

"The tides have been following the same schedule for a lot longer than we've been around. Why would they change today?"

She helps her onto the stones, some of them nearly knee-high, yet to be dried by the sun and wind. Miss Min's feet are mangled; she wears flat plastic insoles in her boots to help her walk. Most of the rocks are sharp, almost crisp, volcaniclike rock. Like the rock she cut her arm on at the bottom of the sea. Each step sends flocks of water bugs scrambling, as if the rocks are moving.

They stand under the *torii* gate; it must be three times higher than they. Miss Min is breathing heavily, the trip across much more of a strain on her. Atop the gate, there is a gathering of stones thrown by somebody. It brings good luck if one lands there. But when? Has their luck changed? Since there is a gate, there must also be a Shinto shrine of some sort.

"I'm going to go over there. Do you want to come?"

"No, I'll stay here. Don't go far. The tide is going to come back soon."

"There is no far to go here, Miss Min. And the tide won't return for more than an hour. I won't be long."

She goes around the shore of the island; it is not marble-shaped as she had thought. When she gets to the south side, there are some large rocks, much like those across the way at the suicide cliff. Light brown, the bottoms wearing slippery skirts of moss.

"Miss Fuji!"

The panicky voice of Miss Min. A few minutes away, she hurries as best she can, and Miss Min is sitting there hugging her knees to her chest.

"What is it?" She is puffing from the short run.

"The tide is coming. The tide."

"That's not the tide; it's from that boat passing by. I told you that the tide won't be returning for more than an hour."

Her tone comes out much harsher than she wants, leaving a hurt look on Miss Min's face.

"Come on, I'll take you back."

They make their way across the almost-dry rocks. She leads Miss Min back to her room, helps her off with her rubber boots, takes the orthopedic insoles out to air them, and, although it is not yet even noon, puts out the futon for her. She is careful to place the soiled side of the futon on the thin straw mats that cover the dirt floor. At least we have the straw mats, she thinks, recalling those early months, when it was the bare dirt floor they slept on. She covers Miss Min's feet with a blanket, reaches underneath it, begins to massage a bit of warmth back into them. She knows that Miss Min feels little, if any, of it at all, but she is past this frustration. Miss Min is talking a little bit about her family and how they were cabbage farmers back in Korea, says she can't even eat cabbage to this day. But she isn't listening to her, only thinking about the island and how it didn't appear as she had thought.

Two weeks later, she returns alone. The pathway opens up in the early afternoon. She retraces her steps from the last time and gets to the place around back where the large rocks jut into a long, narrow peninsula out into the sea. A strange place, the circle part of the island is covered with wild green growth, all of this in the back only bare rock. She takes out a pen and paper and starts to draw. She's never been much of an artist, but still she manages a decent outline of the island. Maps. As long as she can remember, she has always loved them. Would study them as a child, making shapes of dragons or people or whatever. Twisting and turning the maps every which way, creating a different image by doing so.

She continues on around the island; it takes a few minutes to walk. Past the *torii* gate, there is what appears to be a path leading up to the top of the hill. She looks at Nagashima and is surprised by how close it is. Around, in the back of this small island, much of Nagashima is hidden and it feels mysteriously distant. Now, when she turns around, a panorama of Nagashima's east coast is visible: the living quarters, the office, the hospital, the cliff, the small farming area. About the only areas she can't see are the receiving dock, the building where they all spent that horrible first week, and the crematorium—the northwest end of Nagashima, which faces Honshu and the town of Mushiage. She sees a few people walking around in the distance, but she doesn't think anyone sees her. Doesn't believe that anyone pays this place any attention.

She turns her back on Nagashima, takes the path, which is overgrown with fernlike plants and weeds and whatever else. It is only a five-minute hike up, about eighty feet above the sea. Although the day is quite bright, it is dark and cool going through the tunnel of bamboo, maples, cedars. Near the top, she first sees the small shrine, but her eyes are ripped from that when she sees a man sitting on the last of the three cement steps leading to it.

"Mr. Shirayama."

"Miss Fuji. Is this your first time up here?"

"Yes."

"I come up here once a week, or whenever I can get away."

"I didn't think anyone came here."

"They don't. You're the first person I have met here."

She turns around to get a view of Nagashima, but all she can see is the tangle of trees and brush. She turns opposite, but Shodo Island is invisible, as is Honshu, as well as the Inland Sea.

"Wonderful place, isn't it?"

"Yes, it is."

"That's why I come up here. Like a whole different world. You can't see the place, can rarely hear a thing other than your breath, maybe a heron or gull. When I first came up here a couple of years ago, I thought of cleaning the overgrowth, but I realized that this place is special because you can't see anything. Sit down."

She does, and takes notice of the moss growing on the small red shrine, not much taller than she is. The wooden roof, too, has some moss on the north slope, sprigs of grass poking out of its head. There is even a wooden money box to toss in an offering. A couple of dirty one-yen coins lie there. Not their black oval-shaped money, but that of the rest of the country. A churning in her stomach. She hasn't seen or touched this money since her first day here, when it, along with everything else, was taken.

"I don't know whose it is. Maybe belonged to one of the staff."

"Maybe," she answers. There could be a hundred of those coins sitting there, a thousand, and they would be as useful to her as the rocks on the shore. They sit there, two soiled coins, no bigger than a fingernail, and they taunt her. This Mr. Shirayama knows, for they taunted him the first time he saw them.

"What do you think about getting rid of them?"

"Of what?" she asks.

"The coins. You take one and I'll take one and we'll throw them as far as we can."

She regards him, this man, less than five years older than she is, but the disease has taken away much from her image of what he must have looked like before getting sick. He looks back at her; they exchange a strange look, something between agreement and disagreement.

"What's Buddha going to say about us stealing from him?" she asks finally with a light smile. Mr. Shirayama studies her, thinks that she is quite beautiful, the disease hardly touching her, and if he didn't know why she was here, he would not notice anything wrong.

"I think Buddha, or any other god, would understand. We'll replace them with two of our coins. They have more value here. Then it's more contributing than stealing."

She picks up one of the old coins, hands it to him. He takes it, throws it off into the trees. Not much of a throw, but at least it is out of sight. He hands her the other coin. She holds it a short while before placing it in her pocket.

"Go ahead and throw it. You'll feel better."

"I want to drown it in the sea."

They both laugh. It feels good to laugh, makes Mr. Shirayama feel good to share this place.

"What's the name of this island?" she asks.

"Don't know if it has one."

"It should."

"I'll let you give it one, Miss Fuji. I've chosen enough names. What's that you've drawn?"

"A map of this island. Not a very good one, I'm afraid."

"May I see it? I love maps."

"Sure."

She stands up and turns full circle.

"Where's your wheelbarrow?"

"Too difficult to bring up here."

"I can't remember you without it."

"It's good to get away from it for a while."

"What do you grow in your garden, Mr. Shirayama?"

"Mostly squash and beans, some tomatoes."

"Do you like it?"

"I like the fact that I can nurture, bring something into this world. Sort of the same thing that you do, Miss Fuji."

"I don't farm."

"Yes, I know. But when you massage the patients, you bring their bodies back to life for a while. If only in their minds. Sort of the same as farming."

"I guess maybe it is."

She takes back the map, places it on the steps, and puts another piece of paper atop it. She traces another map of the island and gives it to him.

"Thank you, Miss Fuji. I think it's a good map."

"Come on, we must get going before the sea erases our path back."

ARTIFACT Number 0214

A rough, yellowing hand-drawn map
of the small island

She places the sketch of the island on the wall of the room she shares with six other patients. Twists and turns it forty-five degrees every few days until she discovers the shape of it. For many days she thinks, finally deciding on the name: "Key of the Hand Island."

ARTIFACT Number 0230

> Copy of the Order of Culture certificate
> received by Dr. Kensuke Mitsuda—the first
> director of Nagashima Leprosarium—for
> his significant contribution to the arts and
> sciences, November 3, 1951

He wears a black tuxedo, sits in the front row of the state room, along with the four other recipients. When his name is called—Dr. Kensuke Mitsuda—he rises slowly, every movement sharp, as if he has rehearsed them many times. Barely able to bend his feet in the shiny black shoes, he slides more than steps. When he arrives in front of Emperor Hirohito, he puts his arms straight out, perfect parallels, and is handed the medal in a purple velvet–lined box, the linen-lined lid open. He bows his seventy-five-year-old body deeply, holds it there, arms still out, the medal in his hands. Dr. Mitsuda comes out of his bow and retraces his steps, sliding backward one, two, three steps, never turning his back on the Emperor.

ARTIFACT Number 0229

> A bottle of Chaulmoogra oil

She wouldn't remember this; it was before her time. The thick Chaulmoogra oil, extracted from the nut of the Hydnocarpus tree, would course through the patients' veins. So thick, they could feel it. Looking at some of the veins, especially those in the forearm, one could see it crawling through like an earthworm. They dealt with the pain, knowing that maybe, maybe. Sometimes they rubbed their skin with it. Some hoped in those days, hoped that with each worm that crawled through them that piece by piece it would carry the disease away with it. But there were relapses, and the worm no longer provided hope, only pain. Then, six months after Miss Fuji arrived, a new hope arrived as well.

ARTIFACT Number 0231
A whetstone

Every day, observing their bodies, she sees, smells, touches her future. She isn't certain when this future will come, only that, each night, it is a day closer. And it is by the maps of their bodies that she can tell how long they've been here, how much longer until she arrives there. She can do it sometimes with her eyes closed, but at other times she must open them.

The skin:

Seeing the patients laboring with shovels, picks, wheelbarrows, their shirtless torsos bone-dry in the scorching July heat. Several women in their gray-and-white-striped cotton robes working alongside, not a bead dribbling from under their cropped black hair. The Nagashima baseball team, midway through the game, skin dry as charcoal. Massaging a patient, pressing a little too hard, his skin tearing like an onion's, large faults left behind. She remembers the dry, rough skin during the diving season, how her fingertips would split from the cold water and warm air, the stabs of pain when washing the rice before cooking it. Many patients don't budge as she applies the bandages, don't even turn around. Skin hairless, shiny as a polished stone.

The hands:

Fingers like toes, stubs, much of it self-inflicted damage: the man who had a finger ripped off when it was caught in a fishing net being thrown out to sea, how he stared at the air, where seconds before a finger had been; the woman, while making new clothes for the patients, cutting off the tops of two fingers with the scissors; the woman who developed gangrene, her left hand ballooning to twice its size before she went to the clinic and it had to be amputated.

Nearly every time she touches these hands, she is angered, angered at the carelessness; she hates the carelessness—how if they had paid more attention, probably none of it would have happened. And she knows that all she has to do is think back to that time when she cut her arm while diving, how there was no pain; if it hadn't been for the blood, she wouldn't have known about it. Still, there are times when she is massaging a pair of hands—although they have become fewer recently—that she feels irritated. She can tell which of the patients have self-inflicted damage to their hands, which have been destroyed by nerve damage from the disease. Those self-inflicted ones are much more random, a finger or two, parts of them, those from nerve damage much more uniform, a balanced destruction.

The feet:

The woman, who while walking barefoot, sliced her foot on a piece of glass, how she nearly bled to death not knowing of the wound. The orthopedic boots, made and designed by the patients in the woodworking shops, help them to walk, the artificial feet, legs from the knee down. How she sometimes removes these artificial limbs when giving massages, places them next to the futon or props them against the wall. Those who still have their feet, the bend of them collapsing toward the arch, the crinkled, crushed toes. For them, the orthopedic boots, so they don't damage their feet while walking. With the feet, she is much more forgiving, for they are often out of one's sight, self-inflicted damage easier, more understandable, but not the hands.

The eyes:

The young man already wearing the blue glasses, helping to preserve the nerve function of his eyes. Are even the plum blossoms blue? she wonders. How sometimes while giving a massage, she is talking to the patient and he has fallen asleep, but she will talk on for a while, not realizing that the patient has done so, the nerve-damaged eyes never completely closed. No eyelashes, no eyebrows to protect them, the protruding forehead giving them that lion look she has read about from the books on the clinic bookshelf.

The mouth:

Here, patients in the advanced stages of the disease rely on their memories the most. Memories of the taste of a pear; the burn of drinking the freshly made brown rice tea too fast; the texture of a mountain potato; how she wants

to wipe away the spittle that hangs, drips from their un-
feeling mouths.

The nose:

Flat, splayed, twisted, some with nearly none at all, the
septum gone, nothing to hold it in place, collapsing it. With
the worst of the patients, she places a menthol balm under
her nose before massaging them. The overpowering stench
of mucus built up in their noses—the smell of the rotting
flesh is something that even after all this time, all these
massages, she can't get used to. The mucus draining out—
she always has a towel handy to place under their faces
when she massages their backs.

And when she returns to her room, she refuses to allow herself to feel sorry for any of them. She can't allow
herself to do that, for if she does, it will crawl into her in
the form of self-pity, and that, she knows, is also self-
inflicted, also a sign of carelessness.

Her future is somewhere on this island, everywhere,
lurking in each patient she sees who doesn't see her, every
one she touches who doesn't feel her hands, the patients
whom she knows in time she will become. The waiting
more difficult than the actuality.

But her future doesn't come. In her sixth month at Nagashima, she begins receiving her shots and taking her
doses of Promin. The only future that this assures her of is
one of nausea, vomiting, headaches, loss of appetite, wearing a head covering and long sleeves in direct sunlight.
Even this future is unpredictable—sometimes all of these
side effects after taking the medicine, sometimes none, or

a combination of them. Even in this, she has been lucky; others have skin rashes, blood disorders, a bluing of the skin from the medicine.

Months and months pass, and now she can count the months as years. Still she has only the two numb spots on her body—the left forearm, the lower back. Medals or curses—she isn't sure how to wear them. The one thing that keeps her going is knowing that she is not alone, that there are all the others who arrived that same year as she did, several years before, and in the years after. And she is like them. Living here every day in all their outer normalcy, amid all the inner torment.

She has been waiting thirty minutes and is still an hour away from where the nurses sit honing their needles on whetstones. If it were winter or suffocatingly hot, she would have stayed back in the room, waiting for the line to dwindle, but she likes the fog. It reminds her of being underwater, how the sea allows only a little of itself at a time to be exposed; even the sound—where it is coming from, how far away it is—doesn't wholly reveal itself.

Knowing that it is much too early to be doing so, but still, to help pass the time, she begins studying the patients, checking for those favoring their left legs. This morning, because of the fog, she can see only fifteen patients in front of her. She, along with them, all take a couple of steps every minute. It is the stops and starts and all the standing that makes her infected right leg throb. The thought of another needle in that leg is unbearable. She feels the pus oozing through the antiseptic gauze, reminding her that she must stop by the school before beginning her rounds of massages and bathroom cleaning.

The infection in her thigh, the chills, the uncomfortable sleeping position left her with another restless night of sleep. She likes sleeping on her right side, cradling her arms around the pillow, but the pain in that thigh forces her to sleep on her back. This is the second infection she has had in the past six months, but this one she endures, recalling the first time and how the nurse sliced open the infected area without using anesthesia. She daubs it each night with cream and wraps it in the reused gauze.

The trees have nearly undressed themselves of the fog by the time she reaches the entrance of the building. Behind her are another five, six hundred patients. She has spotted a woman favoring her left leg and she keeps an eye on her until they enter the building. She steps out of line, checks where the nurses are positioned, walks over to the woman, asks her if she would like to switch sides. They do, and now she waits on the far left side of the four lines.

The air is stuffy, full of the familiar smell of medicine. Four nurses, a line for each, two patients per nurse, per minute. They scrape, scrape the needles over the whetstone, plunge them into the bottle of liquid Promin, patients expose their thighs, needles inserted, pulled out, the patients move on, scrape, scrape the needles over the whetstone, plunge them into the bottle of liquid Promin, patients expose their thighs, needles inserted, pulled out, the patients move on, scrape, scrape the needles over the whetstone. She is nearly put to sleep by the repetition, but she moves step by step, and when it is her turn, she lowers the left side of her loose cotton pants, hears the scrape, scrape of the needle against the whetstone, sees it plunge into the bottle of liquid Promin, feels the pinch as it goes in, comes out of her thigh, and she moves on.

There is little reminder of the fog when she goes outside; all but the very top of Key of the Hand Island is once again visible. She walks toward the schoolroom to get some clean gauze and knows that, for yet another couple of days, her future is frozen, while at the same time another day is about to pass her by.

Before entering the school building, she stands off to the side of the path, in a patch of bushes, and starts to unravel the bandage on her right leg. It is wet and sticky with pus and a little blood. She knows that without the bandage, the pus will stain her pants, but it is the privacy—not so much needing to be alone while exposing her leg, but the need to be alone with her pain—that she seeks. The much-used bandage sticks to her thigh more and more with each lap that she unravels. She wants to scream, to cry, but she concentrates on a bird she has spotted in a tree, bores into it for strength. When the bandage is finally off, she gives her body a little time to relax. She is sweating a cold sweat, wants to sit down. The day has hardly begun, she tells herself, way too early to think about resting. She forces herself toward the school building.

Most are sitting on the floor of the schoolroom, stretching and smoothing out the antiseptic gauze, when she enters. They are here every morning, this soon to be the first graduating class of Nagashima High School, and they remain for lunch, then for their three hours of classes. They work with care, the correct amount of tension when stretching the tears in the gauze, the difference between having to cut the gauze in two, losing a foot or two of the material, or squeezing yet another day of existence out of it.

She doesn't like coming here, feels uncomfortable among the educated, she herself having attended only seven years of school before beginning her diving at the age of sixteen. She arrived a few years too early to attend school, which only started here last year. Now, although she isn't all that much older than they are—five, maybe six years—she feels much the elder in this room.

Trying not to draw attention to herself, she goes directly to the corner where the rewrapped gauze and bandages are stacked. But he sees her; she knows it before he even speaks, as if he were waiting for her.

"Good morning, Miss Fuji."

"Good morning, Mr. Yamai," she says, continuing in the direction of the bandages, hoping that they will only exchange greetings.

"I didn't see you getting your shot today."

"I was a little late."

"Your leg isn't any better." He points at the bandage in her hand. She wants to toss it away, but she sets it in the laundry bag that Mr. Yamai has come to collect. She picks up a new bandage and tries not to walk too fast out of the room. Mr. Yamai, with the laundry bag flung over his shoulder, follows her. When he catches up, he secretly hands her another bandage, which she quickly thanks him for, shoving it in the left pocket of her jacket.

"I hope to see you on Sunday night, Miss Fuji."

"I don't think so, but maybe sometime when my leg is feeling better."

"Miss Min will be telling a story this week, and this month we'll be reading some of Natsume Soseki. It will be a good time to attend."

"I can't promise, but maybe if my leg is better."

"I *hear you* are telling a story this week, Miss Min."

"Yes, this week is my turn. Did Mr. Yamai tell you?"

"Yes. Why do you know?"

"Because he wants you to come some night."

"I've told you what I feel about going to those kinds of things."

"It's only people telling stories and reading from books. It's mostly done for those of us who can't see well enough to read ourselves. Mr. Yamai is a nice young man. He's about your age, isn't he?"

"You sound like a mother trying to marry her daughter off, Miss Min."

"A lifetime is much too long to be spent alone."

Although her leg hasn't improved all that much, she goes on Sunday night. She is surprised by the number of patients who have gathered. In the back of the large room, she finds a cushion and sits. It isn't long before Mr. Yamai steps to the front and the voices immediately hush. A studious man— maybe it is the round black-framed glasses, or the fact that he is a teacher at the Nagashima School.

"I'm glad that all of you could make it tonight, and I'd like to welcome the first-timers." He looks her way and stops for a second. "Tonight we will read several of Natsume Soseki's short stories. If any of you have any suggestions for future books, please tell me. Before we read from our book tonight, we will have a couple of stories told by Miss Min."

Mr. Yamai stops talking while the room fills with claps. She searches for Miss Min but doesn't see her at first, not until the patient next to her points to the right of Mr. Yamai. Miss Min is sitting in a chair, her shy smile deflecting the clapping. She thinks of all the massages she has given Miss Min, and her often talking during them.

"For those of you who haven't joined us before, this is Miss Min's seventh time to tell us stories. Okay, Miss Min."

Again there is clapping, and Miss Min stands up and gives a bow, sits back down, and then the room is silent:

Out of a single giant cedar they carve the prau, four village men long. From early in the morning, when the young girl came down with the fever, and for the whole of the day and all of the night, the villagers work.

It was this way five years before, when the man's skin burst out in blisters—the prau worked then—only the man died, and the village was spared. Six years before that, when a young woman returned from the jungle, foaming at the mouth and crazed, then, too, they had be-gun to build a prau, but they stopped when her mother found the puncture wounds of the viper on her daughter's left shoulder. The demons hadn't sent disease their way, only the normal strides of nature. But with this girl and the fever, they knew they had to get the prau built and sent off as soon as possible.

As the women work on the image of the man, creating him from husks, tree bark, palm leaves, the men hollow out the insides of the tree. Children feed the workers, whose hands are too busy to stop. They turn their heads away from the work only long enough to have some water poured down their throats, atop their heads. The village elder comes to the shore.

"Fever's getting higher."

He turns and heads back to the hut where the girl burns away. Hands mold the man-doll faster; machetes fling the red insides of the tree onto the sand; children stack fruit and gourds of water alongside.

It isn't until the banana of a moon has crawled halfway across the roof of the island that the village elder reappears.

"The demons have taken her."

The workers pause to offer a prayer for the girl. The fires made by the children light the way for the finishing touches on the prau.

They wait until the tide begins to walk away from the shore, then launch the boat, running alongside, pushing it until the water reaches their necks. Several boats follow the prau, urging it along, making certain that it doesn't turn back to Buru Island. On the shore, the villagers are chanting: "O sickness, go from here, turn back. What do you want here in this poor land?"

In three days, they will return to the shore and kill a pig, offering part of the flesh to Dudilaa, who lives in the sun, and the village elder will recite a prayer: "Old sir, I beseech you make well the grandchildren, children, women, and men, that we may be able to eat pork and rice and drink palm wine. I will keep my promise. Eat your share and make all the people in the village well."

But on this night, after the long day, the villagers, when the prau is out of sight, still do not rest. They go back to the village and prepare to bury the young girl whom the demons have stolen from them.

Miss Min stops and takes a drink of water handed to her by Mr. Yamai. She straightens herself in her chair and begins the second story:

Awake, before the call to prayers, the naked young boy is looking at the prau, which has washed ashore during the night. The once-recognizable man-doll is wet and beaten, but still intact. The two-month journey has left the sail in tatters; the anchor lies next to the toppled prau; somewhere in the Seram Sea the oars have been lost. The boy picks at the seaweed caught up in the large doll.

The sky to the east of Manipa begins to lighten ever so slightly. This is when the screams of the village elder shatter the sleep of every villager. Not like the call to prayers, but haunting, deep from the guts. Screams, the villagers know before they are even out of their thatched huts, that will leave things different for quite a while, maybe for their lifetimes.

The village elder is dragging the boy away from the prau when the others arrive. There is enough light now to see the outline of the prau, to know what has happened, what has to be done. Whatever sickness has been sent away from one of the surrounding islands, whatever has been sent, will have come on this prau, has maybe already spread to the villagers while deep in their sleep.

No one goes near the young boy. Not even his parents, his sister held back by them. Before the morning sun kisses the sea, the villagers have the prau burning, huge sparks flying off into the sky, the villagers standing back but looking, hopeful that the demons will be chased away by the flames, chased away from the village, the island.

Alone, later that morning, the village elder questions the boy.

"When did you first see the prau?"

"When the morning star was still bright."

"Do you feel sick?" He is touching the boy, feeling his head, neck.

"I feel fine. A little hungry."

Staring into the boy's eyes, he asks, "Did you touch anything in the prau?"

"Only the doll."

"Tonight, and for many nights, you and I must sleep away from the village."

And that night, while small pieces of the charred re-

*mains of the prau are being carried away by the high tide,
the villagers try to sleep. But once again, the village elder
wakes them from their restlessness. It is not the terror-
filled screams of that morning that awaken them. It is the
village elder, who sleeps with the boy away from the beach,
near the jungle; it is his hacking cough, which he tries to
smother in his sleeping mat, that keeps them up on this
night.*

ARTIFACT Number 0487
A tube of burn cream

She isn't sure why, but she knows beforehand that she will
do it. Maybe for attention, but to her that seems too obvious an answer. To understand the patients more maybe, but
that seems too noble. It is in the middle of her two-hour
night shift to keep watch and she is the only one in her
wing of the building who is awake. She knows that in each
of the rooms all over Nagashima there is at least one patient awake at this hour—closer to dawn than dusk—a
stick or pipe in hand. A candle burns on the windowsill and
she gazes at it. She has had a bad day, all the massages, the
humidity, the homesickness for the sea. It is mid-June; the
water has begun to warm for the divers.

In each of the rooms, there is a carpet of futons at
night. Six in her room, seven patients. Not enough futons
to go around, but also not enough floor. She is startled out
of her thoughts when she sees the two green dots reflected
in the light of the candle. She is quiet as she crawls in the
direction of the beady, glowing eyes. It isn't on any of the

futons, but at the entranceway, so if she does it correctly, she will not have to wake any of the patients in the room. She is about five feet away, holding her breath, making sure of which way the candle throws her shadow, a piece of the cardboard box beside her. She reminds herself to aim behind the eyes, she does, and when the large stick comes swooshing down, she knows that she has at least stunned the rat, if not killed it outright. She hits it again, prods it to see if it is alive, and when it doesn't move, she guides it onto the piece of cardboard with the stick and carries it outside. In the wooden box, there are two other rats; she drops this latest, along with the cardboard, into the box, which will be burned in the morning.

The end of her shift is near when she goes back inside, but even when she is replaced by one of her roommates, she knows she will not sleep deeply. It isn't because of any fear of the rats that she can't sleep, but the killing of it has now sparked her senses. She knows that what has happened to some of the other patients will never happen to her, or if it does, it will never get too far. There have been only two cases of rabies since she has been here, and she knows that the minute that she would feel the biting, she would awaken, scare the rat away. But it isn't rabies that has started them doing night watches; it is for the other patients, the ones who came to Nagashima before her, those years before the Promin, those whose nerves in their limbs have lost feeling. It is for them that they sit awake and protect.

The night watches began not long after she arrived—when Miss Furato, two buildings down from hers, had two fingers on her rotting left hand eaten away by a rat while she slept. This happened even after the prior winter, when they started sewing stones into the corners of the worst-off patients' blankets, weighing them down, keeping their hands and feet from slipping out from under the blanket while asleep, not so much to protect them from rats as to keep them from being exposed to the below-freezing temperatures. Winter nights knife through the futons, settling like cold, cold tofu. If she stays in the exact place, her body warms up a little, but an inch outside of the fringe of her body's imprint, ice, freezing her all over again.

No matter how bad the winters are, she hates summers the most; how the futons get all moldy. She can't remember a time at Nagashima when they were ever like they were supposed to be. Can't remember a time when they were like they were after a day hanging out in the sun to dry, beaten to a fluff with a stick, sinking into one at night, her body an inch or two higher off the floor.

Besides the futons, the bugs are the big problem in spring, summer, and autumn. Of course there are cockroaches and those microscopic ticks that invade a futon and leave you with itchy, painful bites all over your body, but it is the centipedes that trouble her most. Finger-long, with pincers that leave a poisonous bite behind—some of the bites swelling up to the size of a tangerine. And on her night shifts, she keeps an eye out for them as much as for the rats, has whittled one end of the yard-long stick into a sharp point with which to stab the centipedes. Difficult to kill, have to chop them into three separate pieces.

It is time now to awaken Miss Kato to replace her on

night watch. She reaches over, takes the candle from the windowsill, tilts it over her arm, drips the hot wax onto the spot on her forearm, keeping inside the numbness of its borders. The wax hardens and she peels it off, careful not to break the waxy mirror of her spot. She sets the hardened mold on the windowsill, bends over the candle, this time holding her forearm over the flame, playing with the flame, making it stretch, lunge at her arm. She allows the flame to touch the spot, smells the singeing of the skin. How long can she hold it there before she feels something? How deep does this numbness go? Could I burn a hole all the way through my arm and out the other side without feeling anything? she wonders.

The stench of the burning flesh, not pain, makes her pull her arm away. Her forearm is a mess, the color of the inside of a dried fig. She places the candle back on the windowsill, next to the waxy fossil of her spot, then goes over and rouses Miss Kato awake.

ARTIFACT Number 0400
A map of the town of Mushiage

She has lived through four winters at Nagashima and it is her fourth summer here when the first of the two visitors she will ever have arrives. The young woman sitting across from her bears little resemblance to her. If one looks closely enough, there is something in the shape of their mouths, the slightly protruding upper lip, that hints at family. Nothing more.

The older sister talks in a soft but high-pitched voice.

Perhaps constricted by her nervousness, or maybe that is how her voice is. Miss Fuji sits there, knowing that this will be the last time that she will ever see her sister.

"You've ruined my life. You deserve to be with all these freaks here."

"There are no freaks here, only people who are sick."

"Sick freaks."

"How are Mother and Father?"

"They are no longer any part of you. None of us are. How could you do this to us?"

"Do what?"

"Humiliate us. People won't speak to us. Everywhere I go, people whisper, point. Father and Mother may have to move. We don't get half of the normal price for our rice. The value of our land has gone down. Like it's infected."

"I'm sorry, but I didn't want this sickness. I never asked for it."

"Neither did we. It's like *we* have it. Last year, I was supposed to marry Yukihiro, and now his family has put a stop to it. Because of you. And you made it all the worse when you went and hid. Then everybody found out, the whole island. The police came and searched our house and the fields. Came back many times."

"And what if I had returned that day? What would all of you have done?"

"At least we could have maybe sent you here quietly, told the neighbors that you went away to live in Tokyo or that you died or something."

They glance at each other for a fleeting moment.

"That's what Father said."

Another glance.

"And I agree with him. Better one dead than the whole family."

"Well, it is as if I am dead. You will never hear from me again."

"Too late for all that. I will never come back here. They made me bathe in disinfectant before I came in here and they made me wear this bodysuit, like I'm the one who's sick. I told them your name and they asked me to describe you. Where were you from? When did you come? As if I haven't been humiliated enough by you, and then they make me go through all that."

Those are the final words the sisters will ever speak. The older sister stands up, leaves the room, and goes back through the disinfectant bath before getting on the boat that will take her over to the mainland, from where she will catch another boat to take her the seven miles to Shodo Island.

Late that night, after her sister's visit, she does it for the first time. That first trip across to Key of the Hand Island, almost three years before, has given her courage to expand as much as possible the perimeters of Nagashima. It is August. The water is the warmest it will be all year. It's late; she stands at the edge of the dock, her dock. It is dark; even the outline of Key of the Hand Island, four hundred yards away, is difficult to pick out. She stares to where she knows it is and, in time, finds it. But when she turns her eyes away and then tries to relocate it, once again she must search.

The moon has already long ago followed the sun over to the rest of Asia.

She slips off her sandals and, without thinking, she's in the water. Hardly a splash or ripple left behind. Within half a second, not a trace. She stays underwater for a third of the way—it isn't all that far—the shore not much more than one hundred yards at its farthest point, and at other places, half that. A few years ago, she could have made it the whole way across on a single breath.

Twice more she goes under; her lungs have lost much of their strength, not because of the disease so much as that she is out of practice. She tries judging the shore by the sound of the scallop farms clicking in the water, but she doesn't do a good job of it, scraping her chest and stomach against the bottom of the shore. The other shore. The shore of Honshu. The town of Mushiage.

She walks the stony beach, sits at the edge of a wooden dock. She has to catch her breath, not only from the swim but also from the realization of where she is. The other shore. How easy it was. The realization that she could run away is nearly too much for her. Run as fast as she can. She has about five hours before dawn. How far away could she be in five hours? Twelve, fifteen miles? She does a quick calculation, then laughs at herself. Where does she run? Whom does she run to? She has no clothes other than the thin cotton robe she wears, no shoes—her sandals are back on the dock—no money. No chance. Like the few others who have tried. One patient, three years ago, drowned in this very channel. Several others were caught, and after spending a long time in the isolation building, they were paraded past the other patients, searing, mocking into their memories not to try it.

It isn't all that long before she is dry. August, even past midnight, is hot enough to dry her. Across the way, only darkness, barely a trace of Nagashima. Everybody is deep in sleep over there. The fishermen are still an hour or two from awakening, over here. She is alone. No one in this country knows where she is. This thought alternates from ecstasy to anxiety. The most freedom she has felt since her diving days. Lifetimes ago.

The dock moans and groans, following her all the way to the land. She feels the sting on her stomach and chest from where she brushed the rocky bottom of the shore.

It is a small town; she can tell that even in the dark, even after walking only a couple of minutes. Her bare feet are tender against the cement. It is not any different from other fishing towns she's been to. Except now, at this hour, there are no people. She goes along the main street. She hears to her right the soft lapping of the tiny waves. She passes a noodle shop, a market, which, she can tell from the smell, is for seafood, a couple of other little shops, a few houses. Everything asleep, all within hearing and smelling distance of the inlet of the sea. So quiet here. Up the street, there are two buses parked—MUSHIAGE BUS CENTER reads a sign. She checks the small schedule in front, a bus every hour and forty-five minutes. One to Oku Station, the other to Hamanaka.

She goes to the port, sees dozens of fishing boats nudged by the water, dancing out of rhythm with one another. Small boats, for two or three people. The whiteness of their skin glows in the night. On one of the boats, a man looks like he has just awakened. Ten yards from her, a small kerosene lantern showing the outline of his frenzied hair. He looks at her; she's not sure how much he can see, but he is looking. She doesn't budge. When the flame of the lantern is jiggled by the wind, she realizes that she shouldn't be here. She starts to run, away from the man, his boat, lantern, his wild hair. When she gets to the main street, she has to stop and think which way to turn. Left and down the street, passing, she's certain, the houses, market, noodle shop—sees none of them. She is at the small dock, not sure how far from the man. Hundred yards. Three feet. Can't be all that far. She doesn't pay any attention to the creaks she is awakening on the wooden dock, she gets to the end of it, slips herself into the August water, goes under, and points her head toward Nagashima.

ARTIFACT Number 0243
A photo of the Mushiage-Nagashima ferry

He, as was true with so many of the patients, had had his last moment of freedom on this shore of Mushiage, the same dock, not far from where she now sits on this late night, where the ferry brought them across the channel. The same dock that he would have stood at on the day he arrived in Mushiage at the age of fifteen. The dock where an official from the leprosarium marked his footprints, preventing others from stepping where he had walked.

She has learned not to ask Mr. Shirayama of the days before his arrival, because, although he talks openly about every detail of his years here, he is guarded, protective of his days before Nagashima. As if he has dripped water on that salty mound of his memory and allowed it to dissolve grain by grain. Once, she asked him what his real name was, and when he didn't respond, she thought he hadn't heard, so she repeated the question. He glared at her and still said nothing. He glared at her until she turned away.

But, after almost four years of knowing Mr. Shirayama, he has told her some things, or at least allowed them to slip out. It was in 1939, eight years after they opened this facility, nine years before she arrived here, that Mr. Shirayama traveled nearly a hundred miles by freight train, and then, from the station, walked the remaining twelve. It was spring, most of the way a slight grade down toward the coast, from where he took the ferry the final five minutes here.

Unlike herself, he hadn't hidden from the police. His parents had delivered him to them. That is all he has ever told her of his years with his parents—they never looking back at him as they left the police station. Still, to this day, it is their backs that he remembers, and the huge burden he placed on them. He was a disgrace to his family, neighbors, town, a fifteen-year-old boy who stoked unmentionable fear into others, one who had become a burden to the country's expansionist dreams, and the wars that were a part of it.

Burden. That one word damaged him more than the disease. Burden—those little mites that gather in your tatami mats, in your futon, the splinter deep under your finger—

something that you can go on living with, but with nearly every move, you are reminded of it. The constant reminder from all those people around you about how much better their lives would be without you. Subtle and sometimes not so subtle reminders. Sighs. Stares. Rushing their children away when you pass nearby. Whispers. Pointing. He was, still is, he once told her, that mite in your tatami mat, that splinter burrowed in your finger.

These are the few scraps of his life before coming to Nagashima that she knows, and she wishes he would tell her more. But she, too, has her secrets, things she has never told him, anyone. How this shore, for instance, across from Nagashima, is, at night, hers.

ARTIFACT Number 0198
    A calligraphy brush

All through the winter, she watches his breath as he paints.

Man, forty-five. Boy, seventeen. Woman, thirty-five. Man, fifty-six. Man, forty-four. Woman, fifty.

Sometimes, she can stand for as long as ten minutes before he acknowledges that she is there. She isn't sure whether this is because of his deep concentration or his eyesight, which has nearly abandoned him. His face, inches from the surface. Inches from the slender brush, bristles bunched tightly together by the black ink, which has left miniature footprints on his glasses. He doesn't have much of a surface to work on, the urn about the size of a small canister for storing green-tea leaves, smaller than his hands. Not much left after you burn a body for a couple of hours, she thinks. No matter how big the person, all about the same size when a pile of ash.

Watches his breath as he paints.

Girl, nineteen. Man, thirty-nine. Boy, sixteen. Man, fifty-five. Man, forty-three. Man, fifty. Woman, twenty-eight.

It takes him about thirty minutes to paint each urn. An hour or two on some days. Then, for a week, none at all. She imagines that he must have been working nonstop back in 1934, when the Muroto typhoon crushed this area. More than 180 urns needed that late September. Patients, staff. The raw beauty of typhoons and how they don't discriminate.

His breath as he paints.

Woman, forty-six. Man, forty-two. Man, fifty. Woman, fifty-one. Man, fifty-five. Man, forty-one. Man, forty-seven. Woman, fifty-nine.

A kerosene heater at his feet. Sometimes he bends over and warms his hands near it. The hands, which, when he laughs and claps them together, clap only with the heels of the palms, the stumps of his fingers never getting involved. He twists his wrists side to side, up and down in front of the heater. Does this for a while, and then his breath appears once again when he moves away from the heater and back to the table.

Man, fifty-one. Girl, eighteen. Man, forty-eight. Man, forty-two. Woman, forty-one.

He was one of the first patients back in 1931, and he started painting when, later that same year, Mr. Nakahara, the original painter of urns at Nagashima, died. He pushes his thick glasses against his twisted face and squints real hard before acknowledging her for the first time.

"One thousand two hundred and fifty-one."

This is how Mr. Oyama, the Nagashima urn painter, greets people. Says this as he works his way around the grounds in his wheelchair, or in his room when you enter, or here in this shack outside the crematorium. And for the rest of this day, he will greet everyone with "One thousand two hundred and fifty-one." Unless, of course, someone dies; then his greeting will have a number added to it, but only after the urn is painted.

He turns back to his table, and today, like all the days of the past week, it is slow. He has two lines of urns, six in one row, four in the other, and one by one he paints them.

Man. Man. Man. Man. Man. Man.

Woman. Woman. Woman. Woman.

He prepares for spring, which begins tomorrow, and it will be two months into it that she will turn twenty-four. Half of her urn is already answered; all he has to do is wait for her final number before he must paint.

ARTIFACT Number 1002
A pair of rubber boots

His feet, nearly white, the skin like jellyfish, loose and falling off, leaving large patches of raw flesh exposed.

"When are you going to ask for those rubber boots, Mr. Yamai?"

"I know I have to, but the administrators don't like us asking for things that are so basic. Besides, I don't think they like the things we have been doing with the readings and stories."

"But it's only a pair of boots. Other patients have boots."

"Those are the orthopedic boots. It's as if they are punishing those of us whose disease hasn't progressed."

"Go and ask for the boots."

ARTIFACT Number 1012
          From the bookshelves at Nagashima

Pai Miu is sick. The Master went to see him and, holding his hand through the window, exclaimed, "Fate kills him. For such a man to have such a disease! For such a man to have such a disease!"

—sixth century B.C., China, when Pai Miu, a disciple of
Confucius, dies of what is believed to be leprosy

1. Those suffering from *ta feng* have stiff joints;
   the eyebrows and beard fall off.
2. The wind scatters throughout the muscles and
   comes into conflict with the *wei chi,* or defensive
   force. The channels being clogged, the flesh
   becomes nodular and ulcerates. And because of
   the stagnant movements of this defensive force,
   numbness results.

3. The vital spirits degenerate and turn cloudy,
   causing the bridge of the nose to change color and
   rot, and the skin to ulcerate. The wind and chills
   lodge in the blood vessels and cannot be got rid of.
   This is called *li feng*.
4. For the treatment of *li feng,* prick the swollen
   parts with a sharp needle; let the foul air out until
   the swelling subsides.

—from *Nei Ching* by Huang Ti (600 B.C.)

- garlic used with marjoram cures the lepras;
- mustard with red clay is used against the lepras;
- nettle in wine cures the facial lepras;
- wine sediment is rubbed in against the lepras;
- boil the root of scammony in vinegar to the consis-
  tency of honey, with which the lepras are rubbed;
- fat of the porpoise carries away the lepras.

—ancient folk medicines for leprosy

Patients were segregated in leprosaria in Europe in the
Middle Ages. Leprosy became know as "the living
death" where funeral services were conducted when a
person contracted the disease declaring their death to
society. Leprosy sufferers had to walk on a particular
side of the road, according to the direction from which
way the wind was blowing; some areas required them
to wear special garb, wear a declaration sign around
their necks and to ring a warning bell announcing that
they were "lepers" from which people should flee.

Other discriminating laws of the church and state required that use of separate seats in churches, separate holy water fonts and in some cases in Britain they had a "lepers' slot" in the church wall through which the "leper" may view the communion service but not "contaminate" the service by his or her presence.

—from *Leprosy in Theory and Practice,*
by Drs. R. G. Cochrane and T. Frank Davey

The WHO—at the fifth International Leprosy Congress in Havana, Cuba in 1948—recommends that sulphone (Promin) should be a major treatment for leprosy. It is accepted that temporary isolation might still be necessary, although for infectious cases only. The committee suggests that ambulatory and domiciliary treatment could be safely and satisfactorily given to most patients. Leprosy has ceased to be a "special" disease, and has simply become a disease for which early diagnosis and treatment of cases were recognized to be essential.

—from World Health Organization reports

It is necessary to have laws which make it possible to force leprosy patients to be contained in sanatoria even if it is against their will. Sterilization is a good way to ensure that the disease will not be transmitted among family members. To escape from a sanatorium should be made a crime for patients and as such be punished.

—Dr. Kensuke Mitsuda, testifying before
the House of Councilors' Public Health Committee, 1951

ARTIFACT Number 0983
An old map of Honshu

The last visitor she will ever have comes in the spring of her fifth year at Nagashima.

She appears nervous, perhaps still stinging from the memories of her sister's visit the summer before. They sit in the same room, at the only table. Her uncle Jiro is a short, compact man, much more like her than her sister.

"How are you feeling?"

"I feel fine. I do."

"You are no different from the way I remember you. How long has it been since I've seen you?"

"New Year's, six, maybe seven years ago."

"Your mother and father say hello."

She knows this isn't true, knows that her parents are unaware of this visit, knows it more than anything in her life. Still, she manages.

"Thank you. I say hello, too."

He says nothing. She looks at him and remembers, leaving traces of a smile.

"What are you thinking about?"

"About our trip to Mount Fuji. It is one of my best memories of . . ."

"Of what?"

She turns away before answering.

"Just one of my best memories."

"I went again last year and I often thought of our trip there."

And they return to their silence. Maybe at this moment, he, too, is thinking of that trip more than a dozen years before. She is.

The year she turned nine, he had promised to take her with him on his triennial climb of the country's greatest mountain. The year she turned nine. It was her first time on a train. First time ever, even to see one, other than in a picture. The trip was long, most of the day and all of the night, her head resting against Uncle Jiro's shoulder, his against the wooden-shuttered window. She slept little, surrounded by the trundling of the train through the night, flickers of red lights inside the cabin. At first, and for quite a while, she had thought them to be lightning bugs, and it wasn't until her uncle awoke and lighted a cigarette that she realized they weren't.

She was fascinated that all of it, all that she had seen during the day and all that had passed unseen in the night, was her country. Startled her. So much more than the sixty-square-mile, galloping headless horse–shaped island of hers. Her uncle had bought her a map, and as they passed by towns and through stations and cities, she marked the journey. But when the sun rose the next morning, there was a large gap between Yokaichi and Fuji Station. She would not fill in that part until the return trip, felt that until she saw it with her own eyes, during the light of day, saw them actually passing through the towns and cities and stopping at the stations, seeing the signs with her own eyes, that until she saw this, she wouldn't have really been there.

It was not one of those beautiful clear days like she had

seen in pictures of Mount Fuji—a stray cloud hovering majestically over the cone—but cloudy and humid. She could see halfway up the mountain, and her uncle must have noticed her disappointment.

"The weather changes by the minute on Fujisan."

They continued on, but it seemed that the mountain never got closer.

"When do we get to Fujisan?"

"We have been on Fujisan for the past three hours. All of this wonderful farming land here was given to us from the gods of the mountain. We will spend the night up here near the base. Tomorrow, we do the real climbing. More than twelve hours."

They spent the night at an old temple, which her uncle told her was for mountain worshipers. He told her how the mountain was divided into ten stages and it wasn't all that long ago that women hadn't been allowed to climb past the eighth stage. The true climbers of Fujisan loved the mountain, he told her, and they believed that gods and ancestral spirits lived in it—not only Fujisan but all of the mountains in Japan—and they spent all winter inside the mountain, and in spring they descended to protect the rice paddies, and after harvest they returned to the mountain.

"Will we see any of these gods, Uncle Jiro?"

"You have seen them with every rice plant and tree you passed today. They are in here sleeping with us tonight."

Their climb began after a long lunch of barley, mountain vegetables, dried mackerel, and green and brown tea. They climbed and climbed, the view hidden by the trees. She would get glimpses of the sky, a beam of sunlight, but never a complete view. Her initial uneasiness that she was walking on a volcano abated a long time before they reached the timberline at eight thousand feet, seven hours later, night rushing at them. They sat and rested a couple of hours, ate dinner. She was amazed that, after being surrounded by them all day, not a tree was around them. Barren. Rocky. Dark. Lifeless.

"All of this is lava and lapilli."

She wanted to ask what lapilli was, but she let the word dance around in her mouth, liking the sound of it, liking not knowing what it meant, the mystery of it.

"Why isn't it hot?"

"This is an old volcano. There hasn't been an eruption here for more than two hundred years. If you go to the island of Kyushu, you will find many volcanoes that are active and very dangerous. Some of them have gases that can kill people. Fujisan has no gas or steam, no earthquakes."

"It's a big mountain."

"Fujisan is three mountains."

"Where can I see the other two?"

"You can't. We are sitting on Shin Fuji, and its eruptions have covered the other two volcanoes. You must always remember to check below the layers of things to find the truth."

When they began the ascent at the sixth stage, it was cold, and it grew colder and colder, much more than the winter winds off the Inland Sea. But the stars were huge and helped deflect some of the cold from her thoughts. So big and bright that at times they could have been seen through thin layers of clouds. She held her uncle's strong, rough hands—rough as, but not as sharp as, the lava rocks they climbed on. Well before the top, she was more tired than she could ever remember, her legs lifeless. Maybe it was the altitude, so they stopped for a while. Other climbers huffed past them, puffs of breath seen as if they themselves were tiny volcanoes emitting steam on this volcano without it. She knew that her father was right, correct when he had told his brother that she was too young and would never make it, only hold him back.

"She'll make it," Uncle Jiro had said defiantly.

If her uncle hadn't placed his knapsack on her back and lifted her atop his, she never would have made it. She knew it then, would know that biting truth for the rest of her days. But he did pick her up, and over the next fifteen hundred feet and two hours he carried her. The weight of the pack pressed her into her uncle's back, his chicken wings hurting her chest, but she dared say nothing, for the pain was far less than the lifeless legs. And he pushed on, sometimes above the clouds, sometimes in them, below them. One of her great memories and disappointments of that trip was how she had believed that the clouds were so puffy and soft, but they turned out to be nothing more than moisture. But when they were below and above her, she could be taken back to those memories, believing they were still puffy and soft, although she knew differently. And how the weather changed so quickly, how it was like she had fallen asleep in September and awoke in February.

He helped her off his back, returned the knapsack to his shoulders, took her hand, and made her walk the final few minutes to the summit. At the top were many people, many more than a hundred. Her uncle pointed out the new meteorological observatory, which had opened the month before. It was still night, stars large as clamshells. Her uncle wrapped her tightly in his arms; she drew warmth from him, despite the wind tearing through her body. It was so quiet up there; few people spoke as the sky began to shed the night. Different layers, shades of blues and reds and oranges. Beams led the sun into morning. Uncle Jiro lifted her, propped her atop his shoulders, and that is how they said a prayer facing the sun—the June 9, 1938, sun. The stars were still clinging to the night above their heads.

"You are closer to the stars than anyone in this whole country."

"What about all the other people, Uncle Jiro?" She pointed around.

"We are also very close, but you are atop my shoulders, so that makes you the closest."

And although she didn't know it at the time, this is the thought that pointed her in the direction of the sea and pearl diving. She knew that she could rarely be at the highest point in her country, but if she dove, she could be lower than anyone else in Japan. And that is what pushed her those few feet farther into the sea than the other divers. Lower than anyone else in the country.

Uncle Jiro had said that he would take her again to Fujisan on his sixtieth birthday, the time when a person's second cycle of life begins. But I am here, she thinks, and it is my twenty-fourth birthday and he is sitting across from me in all this silence. And how old is he? she thinks. Will he still return to Fujisan on his sixtieth birthday even without me?

"Let's go outside for a walk," he finally says to her.

And they do, walking around and down to the shore and out onto the dock, where you can see Shodo Island in the distance.

"Every birthday, I want you to come here to this same spot at eight o'clock and I will give you your birthday present."

She gives him a strange look, but smiles a little, not knowing what he means, but knows him enough to trust what he says.

"This is your birthday present this year." He hands her a small, flat bag.

She unwraps it and turns her eyes to the cement of the dock.

"Thank you, Uncle Jiro."

"You're welcome. I must be going now. Don't forget, next year on the same day, be here at eight o'clock."

"I'll be here."

Still, she can't look at him, her eyes on the map of their trip to Mount Fuji; the ink has splotched a little. The map she had on her wall at home, the map that she will go and place on the wall of her room, which she shares with six other patients. And she will move this map to her private room when they are built more than three decades later.

The following year, on her twenty-fifth birthday, she awakes early and goes down to the dock, which faces south, but if she turns ninety degrees to the left, it is Shodo Island that she sees. Her uncle had said eight o'clock, and it isn't much past seven.

It's a nice morning, a little overcast and cool for May. A fishing trawler slips on by. A single fisherman, but she is too far away to read the boat's name painted on the side. If she were on Key of the Hand Island, over on the far side of it, she could read it, but not from here. Maybe it is the man she sees on her late-night swims. If it is, can he see her clearly enough to tell it is she? She turns her back and waits this way until she can no longer hear the boat.

Time passes, with the workers heading down to their gardens; the fishermen of Nagashima have already hauled in their nets, their catch, their journey out into the Inland Sea not as far as most—a few years ago, the local fishermen complained that the Nagashima fishermen were contaminating the waters, and now they are banned from fishing beyond one hundred yards off the shore.

It is past eight o'clock, well past, and still she sees nothing over on Shodo Island. Maybe he forgot, she thinks. But no, Uncle Jiro isn't a person who forgets. He remembers every little detail—dates of all his climbs to Mount Fuji, typhoons that have ravaged the islands of the Inland Sea, earthquakes. He remembered her birthday last year, so why would he forget this year?

Then, she is so embarrassed that she denies that it could be true, denies it, although she knows it is true. Hopes that it is true. Uncle Jiro, while standing here on this very dock last year, never said morning or night, only eight o'clock. She stands there for a few minutes, as if all the patients know what she has done and she is trying to make it appear as if she didn't make a mistake.

The day is long, everything crawls by. Her hands, while giving the massages, feel like stone; the scrub brush on the sinks is like pushing through sand. She gets to the dock early and she has to sit, all the pacing making her even more anxious. Maybe he will come to visit her, maybe bring her family, but she knows this would never happen, and she doesn't want it to. Rarely has she thought of her family, and in those times that she has, it is usually something negative. The sun has long since set; she is feeling chilled, wondering if she has enough time to go back to her room and get a blanket. She probably does, but decides against it, afraid that she will miss whatever birthday present her uncle has in store for her.

The stars have taken their places, the waves sidle against the dock, the water is still May cold. Remembering the beginning of diving season sends a chill tumbling through her. She wraps herself in her arms, studies the almost-vanished silhouette of Shodo Island. And suddenly, there is a spark of light on top of the mountain. While watching the growing flicker, she tries thinking of the mountain's name. Did she ever know it? Does it have one? She doesn't ever recall being atop it. The fire grows larger, and soon it appears as if the bald spot on top of the mountain suddenly has a fiery tuft of red hair. For the flames to reach her here, she knows that the fire must be large, very large.

She can't help but think of the large fire they have on

top of the mountain over in Kyoto every August 16, at the end of Obon holiday, when for three days the spirits of one's ancestors return home to visit. Many families light little fires in front of their houses at the beginning of the holiday to help guide the spirits home, and again at the end of the holiday for their trip back to the heavens.

And now she has a fire, burning on her home island of Shodo, her own personal fire, which will be there for her every May 12. She stands watching it as its light peaks and diminishes slowly until being devoured by the night. Her eyes remain on the place where the fire had been, and now, she imagines her uncle is dousing the hot coals with water and perhaps even sleeping the night up there, making certain that none of the coals escapes and sets fire to the mountain.

ARTIFACT Number 0536
A roll of gauze

It is on a Tuesday, after receiving her injection, that she goes to get a new bandage for her leg, which has again become infected. There is a strange feeling in the room; the younger patients are rolling and mending the used bandages and gauze as usual, but she feels as if their eyes are following her as she passes. And the strangeness continues when she collects another bandage and Mr. Yamai isn't there to greet her, to hand her another one secretly, as if it were a gift. She wishes he were here; she wants to tell him that she enjoyed his reading and that she is looking forward to next week's tanka poetry night and the second half of *Snow Country*. She walks out of the room, and before she is down the steps, there is a soft voice.

"Miss Fuji."

Turning to where the voice comes from, she sees a young girl, one of the high school students. She walks to the side of the building and the girl looks around nervously before speaking.

"They took Mr. Yamai away last night."

"Who?" she asks, although she doesn't need to.

"Some administrators," the young girl says. "I'm not sure who."

"Why?"

"I'm not sure, but some people said that he asked for rubber boots for the laundry workers."

"He had told me he wanted them. The skin on the workers' feet was tearing from the water they were always standing in."

Their eyes meet, then break away.

"It's not because of the boots," she tells the girl. "They don't like him and his stories; his mind scares them. Thank you for telling me. I have to go now."

The young girl grabs her by the arm.

"Here."

The girl holds out her hand and in it there is a clean bandage.

"I saw Mr. Yamai sneak you an extra one each morning." The girl blushes.

"Thank you." She stuffs the extra bandage in her pocket and hurries away.

ARTIFACT Number 0438
The large bell atop the Hill of Light

She is shaken from her sleep.

"Miss Fuji. Miss Fuji."

She turns over on her left side, away from the person who is shaking her, thinking it is one of the patients, wanting some medicine.

"Miss Fuji."

When she opens her eyes, she is surprised to see Miss Min leaning over her.

"Miss Min, what is it?"

There are others awake in the room.

"It is Mr. Yamai. Mr. Yamai has died, Miss Fuji."

"But . . ." And she stops there.

She goes into the washroom, throws water on her face, and even when she dries off, it feels as if it is still there. While brushing her teeth, she turns and sees several of her roommates near her. She spits into the sink. "I'll be there in a minute."

They give her quick apologetic bows and go back down the hallway. She rinses her mouth, throws more water on her face, runs it through her short hair, more on her face and through her hair. She takes a deep breath, releases it slowly, like she used to do before beginning her dives, thinks of the way Mr. Yamai read that night less than two months ago, the way he held the book with such care, such sacredness. Not sure why, but a line from Yasunari Kawabata's *Snow Country* comes to mind: "Moths, how many kinds he could not tell, dotted the screen, floating on the clear moonlight."

Back down the hallway, carrying the kerosene lantern low, she passes other rooms with people still sleeping. Quickly, she changes her clothes, leaves the building with Miss Min. Mr. Shirayama is outside with another dozen patients. There is no moon; she has no idea if it is yet to come up or has already set. She has no idea of the time. It could be midnight as easily as five in the morning. So quiet as they walk away from the buildings, down toward the Inland Sea, then turning right before they get to it, heading up the small, winding path leading to the top of the Hill of Light. She follows, knowing where they are going but not sure why. It takes about three minutes to get atop the hill and there, in the clearing, is the large bell—the Bell of Blessing.

"Miss Fuji, do you want to get us started?"

Her eyes pass over everybody; she hesitates before approaching the bell, which towers over her, over the hill, the island. She grabs the wooden pole hanging from two large chains, holds on to it for a while before throwing it forward against the giant bell, the sound exploding through the night, devouring the whole country's sleep. And she does it again and again, giving the bell little time to finish before making it bellow out over the Inland Sea. Again and again, she throws the pole at the bell, hoping that the sound reaches Shodo Island, wakes up every last person over there. Wakes them and doesn't let them back to sleep until she herself goes to sleep. She continues pushing the pole into the bell until she no longer can. Covered in sweat, she steps aside, and it is Miss Min who takes over the ringing.

There is a line halfway down the hill, and she goes to the end of it and stands. Miss Min joins her in line and they wait, listening to the bell and to one of the patients reading aloud from *Snow Country*.

And for the next three days, the line never shrinks, only lengthens, and the bell rings. Rings while they sleep and stand in line waiting for their injections and eat and while the high school students mend and roll the bandages and gauze.

ARTIFACT Number 0596
A bar of soap

If, at low tide, she stands up to her knees in the water, she can get within fifty yards of the boy and girl. She comes here to forget about the aches within her aches, forget about all the massages she has given, all the patients she has helped over to the toilets, held there, cleaned up after. She comes here sometimes to remember that she, too, is a patient, not that she ever feels like one. The medicine that she takes reminds her of this, but little else.

Like most days, her arms feel like they did after a day of diving, only this tiredness has come from someone else's doing, not from her choosing. Two very different kinds of tired. So when she has some time, here in early summer, she goes to the western shore of Nagashima, the closest point to the main island and the town of Mushiage. The shore, which is covered with large rocks, pieces of wood from the docks that were shattered by a typhoon years back. She has even skipped lunch so as to make time to come here.

Again, today, as she has for the past month, she sees the children playing among the stones, searching for crabs or water bugs or shells. Laughing. From what she can tell, they must be no more than five or six, certainly not any older, for they would be in school otherwise, still a month before summer holiday.

The little boy pulls down his shorts and pees in the water, his sister or friend never distracted from what she is doing. The beauty of it, she thinks, the innocence of peeing without shame. She remembers how for so long when she began diving, she hated, dreaded the time when they all showered after the dives. But in time, she got over it, for the most part.

The boy pulls up his shorts, and before rejoining the girl, he looks across the water at her. Without thinking, she waves. She is stunned, excited by this. He waves back, then returns to his digging. She keeps her eyes on him, hoping that he will again look her way. And in a short time he does, and both he and the girl join in waving. Back and forth, taking turns, as if it is a game, neither of them wanting to let the other be the last to wave. Wave wave. She feels good, giddy almost, and although she knows that as the adult she should let the children win this game, she can't. Can't let that happen.

Almost like those late-night swims and when she sees the wild-haired man on his fishing boat. Fear at first, but then each time she sees him, she will stand and look his way a little longer before running off—if for only a second longer. Someday, she believes, she will speak to him, knowing the enormous risk involved, but also the possibility of the enormous payback of human interaction, whether it be only a couple of words, a smile, a wave. Wave. And she is still waving even after the children have turned their backs to her, still waving as she herself turns her back to the shore of Honshu, waving as she pulls herself out of the knee-deep water.

No matter how sleepy she is each night, she works on the bars of soap. If the moon is up, like tonight, she has a little light. Other times, she does it by feel. Maybe only for five minutes, but a little every day. Waiting until the other six patients in the room are off to sleep. She has smuggled the soap out of the storage room, keeps it inside the cover sheet of her futon. She saves the shaved flakes, molds them into a ball of soap so it can be used later.

One night, not long before she is finished with the bars of soap, one of the patients—Miss Morikawa—is lying there, two futons away, watching her. She isn't sure how long she has been doing so, isn't even certain that Miss Morikawa is seeing, with her eyesight so bad, or maybe she is sleeping with her eyes half-open. But she believes that Miss Morikawa is only staring, as she so often does. She turns her back to her and works on the soap a little longer, glancing around, and each time that she does, Miss Morikawa's eyes remain planted on her.

"Go back to sleep."

Still nothing, the eyes on her. Maybe Miss Morikawa wants a painkiller, and she is about to go over to the building across the way and get her one, but changes her mind, deciding that if Miss Morikawa wants it, she at least has to ask. She shaves a few more pieces from the soap, but now she has lost all her concentration and knows that her distraction will lead to a mistake. Miss Morikawa has always been a busybody, and she knows that tomorrow the woman will tell somebody about the soap. In love with being at the beginning of a rumor, throwing it out there, letting someone else take and expand on it. Someone stealing soap, a good rumor.

There are other patients like Miss Morikawa, and on bad days, when she is giving them their massage, she wants to rip their skin apart. Miss Morikawa is in that group of patients that is religious, and that is fine, she has always thought, but it is when they push the religion on her that she has trouble with it. It happens nearly every time she gives her a massage.

"You should find Christ, Miss Fuji."

"Thank you, but I don't need religion, Miss Morikawa."

"He will show you the light through all these horrible times."

"Religion is fine for some people and it helps them, but for me, I don't need it. Diving is my religion."

"But you don't have that here."

She was tempted to tell Miss Morikawa that she has more than she thinks. Wanted to tell her of the night swims, of the children across the way, of Key of the Hand Island. She didn't dare.

"Maybe I don't have diving here, but I have its memories and what it did for me."

"But how do you deal with all that pain you have caused your family? This place, Miss Fuji, is our penance for all of that we have done wrong to our families."

"I have done nothing wrong, Miss Morikawa. We have done nothing wrong. Your massage is over."

And it is this conversation that the two of them had a few weeks ago that she is thinking of while carving the soap, and when she checks on Miss Morikawa and she is still staring, she tells her, "Go back to sleep!"

This time, she speaks too loudly, awaking another patient.

"Are you okay, Miss Fuji?" the patient asks.

"Yes, I'm fine, just telling Miss Morikawa to go back to sleep."

She hides the two pieces of soap under the top corner of her futon, tries to go to sleep herself, but it takes awhile before she does, feeling that Miss Morikawa is still watching her, and waiting until she can tell someone of the soap that has been stolen.

The next morning, she is awakened by one of the patients.

"Wake up, Miss Fuji."

She does, and when she turns over, she sees the other five patients who share the room crowded over Miss Morikawa's futon; her eyes are still open, staring into space. The patients all wait on her for what to do next. She, at times like this, feels burdened by the patients' dependence on her, wants to tell every one of them that she is also a patient. Some of them truly need her, but there are others who use her. She peels the cover of the futon off herself, hating to lose the warmth that she has created in the night, and goes over, bends down, and closes Miss Morikawa's eyelids as far as they can be closed.

Three nights after the cremation, she finishes the soap figures—a fish and a scallop shell. She wishes that she had something to give them some color, but she knows that this is a useless thought. And now that she has finished with them, she knows that tomorrow night she must go.

And she does. To keep the water off the pieces of soap, she wraps them in a plastic bag and laughs at the irony— keeping soap out of water. When she arrives, she doesn't go through town, staying only on a large rock on the shore. She sets the fish and shell on a stone near where she has seen the boy and girl playing. She walks around the shore-line, hunched over, looking for something the children may have left behind, any hint of them that she could take back with her.

Well before sunrise, she wakes and scrubs the sinks and toilets, massages a few of the afternoon patients in the morning, clearing for herself an hour in the early afternoon, when the tide is out. As she makes her way to the western shore, she feels tight, like her chest and stomach and head are in a cramp. Nervous, not about getting caught, but whether or not the children will be playing today. I am like a child myself, she thinks, but shoves this thought aside, allowing the rare excitement to trundle through her again and again.

They are there and almost immediately they see her. Both of them go over to the large rocks where she had sat hours before. The boy and girl hold something in their hands, jumping and waving. She knows it is the soap figures and waves back; after a few minutes, she stops, letting them win the game. It doesn't bother her today, for she knows that when they go back home, they will be taking something of her with them.

Over the next week, she works harder at night, another two soap figures, this time a crab and a star. While giving the patients massages, she has thought about which of the first soap figures the girl took—the fish or scallop shell? Which will she take this time? She hurries to finish them, knowing that in two weeks school will be out for the summer and other children will also be playing on the shore.

Around midnight on the first Wednesday in July, she is done. She can't sleep and knows she probably won't. She steps on the futons, careful not to tramp on someone, quietly leaves the room, slips on her sandals, and goes down to the dock. Placing the figures inside the plastic bag, she seals it tightly with some fishing line and slides into the water. She makes it on two breaths all the way across. Her goal by next summer is to do it on one breath; every day she practices holding her breath, trying to get her lungs back to where they were nine years ago.

The night has a nice breeze to it, and although the water is still cool, it is nearly the perfect temperature. She unwraps the figures. This time, she has used a piece of shaved charcoal to draw eyes and a smile on both the crab and the star. She leaves them on the same rock as the week before, then gives herself a few minutes to take in the air, the night on Honshu. She doesn't stay long, then goes into the water, takes her time heading back, hauling with her, as always, a dense loneliness. When she feels the rough shell-covered cement, she pops out of the water, placing her hands on the top of the dock, lifts herself up, and reaches out for her sandals, but they are not sitting there. They are in the hands of the assistant director, Mr. Itoh.

ARTIFACT Number 0488
A Japanese Communist party badge

None of this she knows, will only learn of it later.

There is a nervous excitement inside the building; the July 1957 heat is pulverizing them. Although there is no known rule prohibiting meetings, they leave the windows closed. The night before, Mr. Shirayama had spoken with a few of his friends, asking them to pass word to as many of the patients as they trust that he wants to have a meeting. Over two hundred patients are inside, those who need to be are carried, their wheelchairs left out back of the building, along with Mr. Shirayama's wheelbarrow.

The meeting begins at 6:30, giving them a little more than an hour of the dusk light to work with. Mr. Shirayama stands before everyone, nervous beyond belief, never having been much of a speaker, although he talks to his crops, and occasionally to the tools in his shed, although he never does that when anyone is around.

His voice gives away his uneasiness and he blurts out what he wants to say.

"First, Mr. Yamai was taken away from here and he died and now Miss Fuji has been locked in isolation."

There is no hint of surprise, which doesn't shock him, for word travels fast around here. Within less than an hour, news can be communicated to all seventeen hundred patients. But the couple hundred in this room don't make a sound, leaving Mr. Shirayama to forge on.

"What are we going to do about this?"

Amid the second round of quiet, he isn't sure what to say, how to continue on. That is when he is saved by Mr. Nogami, a patient who arrived here a few months before Mr. Shirayama in 1939. They have hardly ever spoken to each other in all their eighteen years on this island. Mr. Shirayama has found him to be a deeply bitter man, never able to shake off his bitterness of being here, the burden he has been given in his life. Not that they all don't have their bad days, but Mr. Nogami seems to have a lifetime of them. He tries as much as possible to avoid people like Mr. Nogami because he doesn't believe that he could survive this place were he to allow bitterness to seek shelter within him. He doesn't try to deal with his bitterness; rather, he has forgotten it. It is easier for him to erase those first fifteen years of his life, before this disease, than try to deal with them and the acidic taste that they leave behind. Mr. Shirayama can bear looking at his history through the histories of others; at least it doesn't suffocate him.

As for Mr. Nogami, he believes that he has every right, many justifiable reasons to be angry. It was his mother who came to visit him late in his first year here, and the final thing she said to him was for him never to come home, not even when he dies.

It was he who had enraged so many of the patients on the day of their country's surrender, when they listened to the Emperor's speech. He had stood up and shouted, "Banzai! Banzai! Banzai!" His cheers shocked everyone nearly as much as hearing the voice of the Emperor himself. Still, twelve years later, many have not forgotten or forgiven what he had done. When he stands up and speaks today, Mr. Shirayama is relieved that someone is helping move the meeting along, although he feels some apprehension when he sees who it is.

"We should fight!" Mr. Nogami hollers.

When Mr. Shirayama heard that Miss Fuji had been put into the isolation building, his initial thought was to start up a petition and present it to the administrators. He had thought the idea of a petition was quite radical and was surprised that he had thought of it at all. But then Mr. Nogami said what he did.

"We were brought to this damn place because we are sick, but here we are not being helped, just working day in and day out to keep this place alive while we die." The right side of Mr. Nogami's mouth is always open; spit flies everywhere. His Japanese Communist badge bobbles on his shirt.

"How much is enough? We don't even have the right to vote. How far will we let this go and keep on bowing to these people like they are doing us a favor? We are doing them a favor! Where would all these people be without us? Nowhere. It is we who make their work possible. They exist because *we* are here! And it is time that we take back some of the power we give them, not let them feed off us. Mr. Yamai isn't the first to die because of them. Miss Fuji isn't the first, and she will not be the last, to be locked away in isolation."

There are a few rumbles in the crowd, and Mr. Shirayama can't make out whether they approve of what Mr. Nogami is saying or not.

"Thank you, Mr. Nogami," he says meekly.

Mr. Nogami doesn't sit back down.

"We certainly have the numbers. What is it now, forty or fifty patients to one staff member? Probably more. What can they do, lock us all up with Miss Fuji? Isolate us when we are already isolated?"

From the middle of the crowd, Miss Min stands and speaks up.

"I agree with Mr. Nogami. They can't make anything worse for us here."

Then a strange and surprising thing happens as Mr. Shirayama is about to try to temper Mr. Nogami's and Miss Min's remarks with his petition proposal. A couple of claps come from the crowd and then a few more, until what must be half of the patients in the room are doing so. Mr.

Shirayama tries hushing them, warning that they could be heard, reminding them of the gravity of what they are doing. They only grow louder, and in time, Mr. Shirayama is also caught up in it, and he claps louder than he ever can remember doing, and he hopes that Miss Fuji, in the cement isolation room, half-buried under a sand dune on the eastern end of the island, can hear them and know that it is not only for her that they are doing this but also for themselves.

The second morning after their meeting, hundreds of them meet outside the building they have named the Lighthouse. They gather at the top of the suicide cliff, light some incense sticks, spend a moment thinking of all the lives that this place has pushed over the edge. Some of the patients don't join in, believing that those who took their own lives were weak. Mr. Shirayama has never agreed with that, he has even thought them to be the brave ones, and there have been times, during those darkest of days, when he has envied their courage.

They make their way down to the administrative building, down near where they all spent their first days at Nagashima.

The sun is barely up. They have gathered as many of the patients who have wheelchairs as they could, and they have brought the empty wheelchairs of those who didn't want to come. There are a few dozen wheelbarrows, and eight of the strongest patients spent most of the night carrying the half dozen small fishing boats up from the shore. Everything is placed in front of the administrative building, a thirty-yard maze of patients sitting in wheelchairs, crowded into the boats, sitting in and standing by the wheelbarrows.

The first of the administrators arrive around 7:30. Five men in suits, not yet changed into their white jackets and hats, standing with their white masks on, their eyes conveying their confusion. Standing there. Finally, Mr. Itoh, the assistant director, speaks.

"What do you think you're doing?"

The night before, the patients had agreed not to say a word. Stay there silent, silent as the administrators have been for the past two and a half decades, silent as the government, their families. Mr. Itoh must think that the words alone would get them jumping, scatter them like water bugs, like they have done so often in the past, for he stands there and waits.

"What do you think you're doing?" His voice rises each time and each time it becomes less of a question and more of an order, a command. "What do you think you're doing!"

At first, not speaking is terribly difficult for many of the patients, but as time passes, it becomes their strength, the hundreds of them linked by it, how they bury the screams of Mr. Itoh and his men with it.

One last time, he shouts, then walks away; his men follow.

Mr. Nogami is the first to speak once they have gone.

"The rest of you stay here, stay where you are."

He points to Mr. Shirayama and the other seven patients

who had helped carry the boats, again repeats for the others to remain behind. They cross the hill, past the building where they held the meetings, down past the empty gardens, the shore without the fishing boats, their nets lying unattended. They arrive at the cement-block shack, about the size of fifteen futons, and they break the lock on the door, lead Miss Fuji and the other two patients out from there. They are filthy and stink, shield their eyes from the sun.

"What's happening?" Miss Fuji asks.

"We've had enough," answers Mr. Nogami.

They start to carry the three of them back, but Mr. Nogami stays down there. He has a small sledgehammer and he begins slamming it against the building. His thick glasses have fallen off, and he is blindly hitting and hitting the building. For a while, nothing happens, but then he finally breaks through a part of the wall. He keeps hitting it until several of the patients go over and try to get him to stop, tell him that he is going to hurt himself. When they finally get him under control, they sit him on the ground, take the sledgehammer from him.

It is awhile before they manage to get Mr. Nogami back over to the administration building. The patients haven't moved, still sitting in the boats, wheelchairs, wheelbarrows. Some of them have gone and brought food and water. The better part of the day is spent there, and still the administrators haven't come back. Some of the weaker patients are moved under the shade of the roof, others inside the building; dinner is brought down to all of them.

"We remain until we get some changes here," said Mr. Nogami, who, although weak from all his exertion, still has his determination left.

The sun sets and they stay. Some of the patients sleep on the cement; others huddle in the boats, some remain awake, talking and thinking about what is going to happen. It is well into the night when they hear the sound of a group of people heading their way. Then the flashlights can be seen. They grow closer. Larger. Brighter. The patients say nothing. All those with the flashlights and nightsticks don't say much, either, their white masks standing out in the darkness. They start swinging wildly, hitting bodies, other times a tree, bodies, the boats, bodies, bodies. Wheelbarrows are flipped, bodies flailing to the cement, and beams of the flashlights burst out every which way, all of it going on and on and on. Mr. Shirayama and Miss Fuji have been shoved and beaten back into the hallway of the administrative building. Many of the patients are in there. Some lay injured on the floor; others try fighting their way back out into the night. The injured are tended to; shreds of clothes are used as bandages, as sponges to sop up the blood.

Not until dawn does the damage become apparent. Glass, bodies, splinters of wood, sandals without feet in them, wheelbarrows, a set of broken false teeth, busted boats, crippled wheelchairs, branches of trees. Outside the building, encasing them, police, a large number of them. The administrators, and others nobody recognizes, are talking, pointing at the patients. Every once in a while, one of the patients is taken away, down over the hill to the western shore of Nagashima, down near the receiving dock.

The Promin injections are given as usual by some of the patients. Miss Fuji is down at the other end of the hall, holding the bandaged head of Miss Min.

ARTIFACT Number 0453
A blank white urn

If there is only one in a day, she can get through it. Tells herself, When this is finished, then you are done; it is all over for another day. And maybe the next day there will be none. And maybe the day after that, as well. That has happened before—two, three days, a week even, without having to do one.

In her white jacket, like the doctor and nurses, a white mask like them, the puffy hat that resembles a shower cap, the trash bag—she's the only one with a trash bag—she is made to witness and, at times, even to help with the procedure.

It is on these days when there is more than one abortion that she sees no end, that all that has occurred must be repeated again. The woman on her back, feet in stirrups, the injection of anesthetic passed by the nurse to the doctor, the cone-shaped tools used to stretch the cervical muscle, the suction machine brought over, turned on, all followed by that horrible sound. This is the time when she calls to mind a song, trying to get rid of that sucking noise, the sloshing sound like those men and women who catch loaches in the mud after the tide has gone out, that sound of feet or boots stuck in the mud.

She never meets the eyes of the women while they are on the table. They probably don't even know that she is not a nurse, but a patient, like them. A patient who has been put here in Clinic B because the isolation room has been destroyed and this is her punishment for what they believe was an attempt at escape the year before. They didn't know, still don't know, that she would only swim over there, take a walk, and return. Doesn't matter. She is now the bearer of the message to all: Don't try it.

All she can do is watch the feet of the patient. The feet and all their tension, toes cradled together toward the aches, strangling in the stirrups. But even then, she has to turn away. Sometimes she doesn't even know who is on the table. Tries her best not to know. Wrestling with the trash bag in her hands, she scurries to find a song, any song, pasting her eyes on the floor or wall.

Then she is given the remains and drops them in the bag. The doctor doesn't even look at her. For this, she is grateful. The weight of the remains. She is never sure where or how to hold the bag. If she puts both hands on top, she can feel the weight sway and jiggle in there. If she holds the bag with one hand by the top and one on the bottom to keep it from moving, then she touches it, the mole-size head, the miniature feet and hands. And there are times when it isn't her imagination at work—with those late-term abortions, five, six, even seven months into it, everything is there, legs and arms, but the skull collapsed by the doctor so it can be pulled out of the womb. She waits with the trash bag open until the doctor throws in the placenta; then she closes it and leaves the room. And it is perfectly clear—and, she is certain, takes no imagination whatsoever—that she is a party to the killing.

She wants to run to the garbage bin, out in back of Clinic B, but she knows that she mustn't let them know of the terror that grips her. She walks, lifts the lid of the garbage bin, sets the bag in there. There have been times that the weight has shifted, horrifying her, leading her to believe that the fetus was moving, struggling to get out. Now, no matter how quickly she wants to get rid of it, she sets it in there gently, then slams the lid shut.

On those days, while in the room during the second abortion, she tries imagining that this is a day when there is only one to perform, and that this is that one, but the exhaustion, the crazed exhaustion, tells her this isn't true. Somehow, she makes it back to her room. One of her roommates goes and tells the patients whom she is to massage that she can't. She drops onto the futon, which someone has prepared for her, and she will lie there, hide under the blanket whether it is the dead of summer or winter. It is on nights such as this that she wishes the disease would ravage her, incapacitate her; then at least someone could take care of her, feed her, bathe her, massage her, until it is time to cremate her.

ARTIFACT Number 0357
A wedding band made of seashell

Again, tonight, for the fifth time this week, he sneaks into the room and joins his wife on the futon. They are only three futons away from her, and she pretends to be asleep. She listens to the rustling of the sheets, aware of them trying to keep quiet, when that is the most difficult thing for them to do. She imagines it is like resurfacing from a dive and trying to control her breathing.

Mr. and Mrs. Matsu were married a few weeks back, and that first late night he came into the room, it took her awhile to figure out what was happening. She had noticed the blankets heaving up and down; she had thought of running over to one of the adjoining wings to get some help, not certain what was happening. She knew a little about these things, how the divers used to joke and tease about their husbands and all, but she was only a listener, never a participant, never understanding much of it.

Now, on those nights when he comes into the room, she waits until the blankets settle and then, after awhile, she can fall asleep.

Three months after their marriage, Mrs. Matsu confronts her while she is on night watch.

"I know that you work in Clinic B and what they do there. I am pregnant and I need your help." She leans in close, whispers.

"What do you want me to do?"

"Nothing. I need you to say nothing."

"They'll never allow you to have the baby. Besides, I have no say in the matter."

"If they don't know, then they can't take it."

Mrs. Matsu stares her straight in the eye, the light from the kerosene lantern bouncing her huge shadow on the wall behind her.

"I would never say anything to them. I hate what they are doing, but I have no choice. That is where they have assigned me."

"I'm sorry, I didn't mean it. I know that you have no choice."

"That's okay. Just because you are late-term doesn't mean they will allow you to keep the child, Mrs. Matsu."

"But if I can deliver full-term, then maybe I can keep it."

"There have been babies aborted in the sixth, even seventh month."

"I'm willing to take that chance. I need your help in concealing it."

"You should be okay for another month or two, but after five months, it will be almost impossible."

She remembers some of the pregnant women back home on Shodo Island wearing wide *obi* belts that pressed tightly against their bellies and how they didn't seem pregnant if you weren't paying attention, looking for it. They make one for Mrs. Matsu, and during the fifth and even into the sixth month, the pregnancy is concealed. It helps that Mrs. Matsu was never one to go out all that often; she works in her room, sewing the cotton-padded lining into the quilted uniforms they wear in winter.

Before leaving the room each morning, she checks on Mrs. Matsu, who, although weak, has a glow about her, a glow she never recalls seeing, not only here but even back over on Shodo Island. It is Mrs. Matsu who pushes her through the days at the clinic, particularly on those days when there is a patient on the table and she is given a sack to throw into the garbage bins. On the worst days, she thinks ahead to going back to her room at night, when only a kerosene lantern will be lighted, and how the six women will gather around their secret, touching the taut belly. "Like the skin of a *taiko* drum," one of them says, and they laugh, laying their faces against it, the miracle of feeling the kick of the baby, the sounds inside.

Then, late in the eighth month, it is Mrs. Matsu who is on the table in Clinic B. The tray of medical instruments, cold and heavy no matter the season, awaiting the doctor to come in. When he enters the room, his eyes meet Miss Fuji's, which are the only things visible to each other behind the masks. His eyes tell her that he knows who she is and her connection to the woman on the table. It isn't until this moment—his look as he walks by her, never stopping or slowing his steps, looking directly at her and then over his shoulder as he passes—that she feels fear for herself and Mrs. Matsu. Any hope that she had harbored for this to turn out right is crushed.

Throughout the procedure, her eyes aren't anywhere near the table, anywhere near Mrs. Matsu, not even at her feet, the swollen feet of a pregnant woman. She tries digging up a song, but this time she can't find a single one. She can't even remember the names of the songs; not a note comes to mind. The only thing she remembers hearing, however, is a slight popping sound, like when one of the divers would remove a fin. She thinks that she hears Mrs. Matsu say the lone word "No," but this she isn't certain of, will never know.

More out of habit than awareness, she holds out the bag, turns her head away, waiting for the weight in the bag to tell her it is in there and it is time for her to turn around, open the door, walk down the hallway, out the back door, open the lid of one of the garbage bins, and drop it in there. But there is no weight, only the bag held out until it is ripped from her hands, tossed to the floor all in one sweeping motion by the right hand of the doctor, his left hand holding out the baby as someone would a drowned puppy.

"Take it. Be sure to tell as many patients as you know. This will never happen again."

The baby is in her arms, the deflated, collapsed skull; the doctor walks out of the room, leaving her and a nurse, and Mrs. Matsu, who is still on the table. The nurse bends down and picks up the bag, takes the baby from her arms, and for a slight moment she feels herself not wanting to let go of it, but then it is gone from her arms and into the bag. Then the bag is in her hands, the weight in it telling her it is in there, and it is time for her to turn around, open the door, go down the hallway, out the back door, open the lid of one of the garbage bins, and drop it in there.

ARTIFACT Number 0623
A cherry tree bonsai

She walks across the damp brown blossoms. The cherry blossoms were cheated of their week of beauty, as the heavy rains beat them to the ground only two days after blooming. This is her first time back to the western shore of the island since the uprising.

Many times she has thought of the boy and girl. That is what got her through those days in the isolation room. It was the children whom she thought of throughout the winter, and she thinks of them now.

Cherry blossoms are matted to the driftwood, to the bottom of her sandals. She sees nothing across the way, allowing the maybes to gather. Maybe they have started school, maybe it is too cold for them to play, maybe they have lost interest in playing on the shore, or, after receiving the last set of soap figures and not seeing her return, maybe they gave up on her.

She waits, staying back from the cold water. The tide is up, but it doesn't matter; there is nothing across the way that she wants to get closer to. As she is about to go back, she hears a voice, then a couple of them. She hesitates, thinking it is her imagination or that maybe someone on Nagashima is talking. For a moment, she can't make herself turn back toward the channel. First, a glance over her shoulder, and this leads the rest of her body to follow when she sees them. She is nervous; shards of shyness overcome her. It is only when they wave that she returns theirs. She stands on a piece of driftwood, but this isn't high enough, so she climbs onto a rock. This is better, but not much; the children can be lost, if only for a second, on the choppy channel.

She waves and they wave. It is she who stops first and she who turns her back on them. A strange emptiness settles inside and stalks her all the way to the room, sits in her all evening, gets under the blanket of the futon with her. And she knows that she shouldn't have made and taken those soap carvings over to the children, not the first time or the second. She berates herself for not being satisfied with only waving to them, for having to go and make the figures, her desperation for the boy and girl to take something of her back home with them.

A few days later, she is back and it isn't long before the boy and girl show up. Although the tide is out, she doesn't go to meet it, even up to her ankles. They wave, but for her, the game has lost some of its verve, the jolt of energy it once gave her.

They have waved only a couple of times, back and forth, when she sees someone running toward the children. An adult. A woman. The boy is the first to turn back to the woman, who is now shouting something. When she reaches the children, she grabs them both by the arms. The boy glances back across the water. The woman smacks him across the head, pushes him ahead of her. The woman turns, points back at her, screaming. Words she will never know. Words that she craves and that horrify her.

Before they are out of sight, something strangles her, shoves her away from the shore. She trips, falls, crawls up the edge of the embankment through the weeds and shattered shells and rocks. Runs, stumbles past the clinic, where she is scheduled to work that evening. And although she doesn't realize it at the moment, she will soon be devastated by the reality that the island of Nagashima, for her, has become even smaller today.

ARTIFACT Number 0624
A scrub brush

Across the channel, in a house in Mushiage, a mother has her son and daughter in the bathroom, scrubbing them with soap, hot water, and brushes. She scrubs as much to clean them as to release some of her rage. The children have finally told her everything.

"Satomi, you are supposed to be watching your brother. Didn't I tell you that you could burn your eyes by looking over there? What you have done is so much worse than looking!"

She goes on with the story that her uncle had told her when she was her children's age. A story she never believed all that much, but it gives her some sort of justification for the fear that is choking her. She sends the children off to their room, goes about cleaning the house and the children's and her own clothes with the same vengeance.

She doesn't tell her husband, or anyone in town, what has happened, worries that she and her children, too, will be shunned. She wants to take the children to the doctor's, but she thinks that maybe they will be taken from her.

For many months, she goes about checking her daughter and son after they bathe, telling them that she is searching for dirt left behind from their day of play, while she checks for spots, for a droop of the mouth, a shortened finger. She knows only what little she has seen, has heard, has imagined.

And she goes on living in silence and terror, for she has no one with whom to share it.

ARTIFACT Number 0638
A teacup

The long walk home after a day in Clinic B. When she arrives at her building, she keeps going until she comes to Miss Min's room. She leaves her shoes at the door and enters. Miss Min is preparing the futon when she sees her standing there.

"What are you doing here, Miss Fuji?"

"I don't know. I'm coming from the clinic."

"Do you want some tea or something to eat?"

"Tea, thank you."

While Miss Min makes the tea, two of her roommates leave the room; three others are asleep on the floor.

"Here. Sit down on my futon."

Miss Fuji does, and she stares at the cracks in the wall. Today, she can't create anything in the patterns, just stares.

"It was a long day at the clinic. One of the patients died on the table. She bled to death."

"Who?"

"I'm forbidden to tell any names. I'm sorry."

"I understand."

Miss Fuji sips her tea, still staring at the wall; the other roommates still haven't returned.

"Why don't you lie down a little?"

Miss Min takes the teacup from her and sets it on the floor in the corner. Miss Min covers her with a blanket, her hands stopping and remaining on Miss Fuji's shoulders. The hands are cold on her shoulders, the fingers bent like claws, but Miss Fuji doesn't mind, doesn't resist, for they feel good resting there.

"It was Miss Hashimoto."

"It's okay. Just rest."

Miss Min's hands begin moving on Miss Fuji's shoulders, clumsy, sometimes pressing too hard or not hard enough, having trouble, due to the lack of feeling in her hands. But Miss Fuji says nothing, for this first massage she has ever received at Nagashima feels good, helping to give her a break from the memories of the day.

ARTIFACT Number 0668
A bottle of liquid Promin

It has been days since she has left the room. Her roommates ask her if she is all right, bring her a small bottle of Promin and a needle. They step over her when they place their futons out at night, step over her when they put them away in the morning. She has always been the one to lay out and clear the futons each night and day, and there is some confusion at first, but the other patients manage helping one another fold and stack them. There is talk that she has suffered a relapse, built up a resistance—like some of the patients have—to the Promin. The disease reappearing out of its cave.

It is only after the second Saturday, when she hasn't met Mr. Shirayama at Key of the Hand Island, that he becomes concerned and goes to check on her. Her thinness shocks him. He is horrified to find a bottle of Promin, not yet used, under her pillow.

She recognizes Mr. Shirayama but says nothing. Her

stubbornness has hardly been weakened, as she refuses to be taken to the clinic. She can't go there, and he sees this in her face, so he and her roommates tend to her. It takes a couple of weeks to bring her back, liquids and boiled rice, working up to fish and vegetables. After many days of refusing the drug, she has started receiving it again.

She barely talks. Mr. Shirayama knows how all of them at some time have teetered on this edge. For the next month, several of the healthier patients substitute for Miss Fuji up at Clinic B. Mr. Shirayama goes there and tells them that she has injured her ankle and can't stand. A feeble excuse, but even more feeble is the response: none. So long as someone can work for her.

By the end of July, the first swarm of cicadas have arrived. It is Miss Fuji's first time over to Key of the Hand Island since her breakdown. Usually, they meet at the top; this day, they cross the stone path together. Today, she wants to go around to the other side of the island, not up to the top. There is little activity out on the water; the fishing boats are back at their docks until the next morning. The thrumming of cicadas can be heard here, everywhere, she imagines. She has never found their noise to be soothing; rather, it irritates her. She speaks, more out of need to distract the maddening sound of the insects than out of a wish to reveal what she has discovered.

"I don't think we will ever get out of here. It has taken me all this time to realize this. I think we are here forever."

"Would it be any better over there, on the main island or back home?"

"I'm not saying that things would be any easier. I know that I don't ever want to return to Shodo Island. But sometimes I think I could survive away from here. Go somewhere where no one knows who I am. I think I could make it. I would like to find out if I can."

"I know you could survive, Miss Fuji. You are fine."

He looks at her, and she does look fine, he thinks, but since she started working in Clinic B, nearly four years ago now, she has aged; her eyes have a heaviness to them, still beautiful, he thinks, but a tired beautiful. The way she walks, not as deliberate as she once did.

"There are times when I want to let this thing totally devastate me; then maybe I would feel justified being here," she says.

For the first time, she has spoken this thought. Neither of them talks. Mr. Shirayama wants to tell her that he knows how she feels, but he doesn't. He knows that he couldn't survive out there.

"Have you heard from Mr. Nogami?" she asks.

"Nothing."

"Do you think we will?"

"I don't know. That is one thing I can't bring myself to think about."

"So, what did we get from the uprising?"

"Small steps, Miss Fuji. They have given us mats to cover the dirt floor; they have given back our money."

"But they are still trying to break us, trying to tame any power that we take from them."

The heat devours her; the Inland Sea is breathless. Mr. Shirayama turns his back to the water and points to the top of the island.

"We need to start sharing this island with the others."

"This island?"

"Here. Key of the Hand Island. It brings me, and I think you, too, Miss Fuji, so much solitude, allows us a brief escape from over there. We need to share this place."

"It is not all that big. And what will the administration say of it?"

"The more I think of it, the closer I am to believing what Mr. Nogami said was correct. How we have to use their power and turn it on them, use it to our advantage."

ARTIFACT Number 1830
            Tide schedule for Nagashima, Okayama,
            Japan: 34.70° N, 134.30° E

05–20	04:43	First Quarter Moon
05–20	05:17	3.24 meters High Tide
05–20	11:40	1.56 meters Low Tide
05–20	17:15	2.62 meters High Tide
05–20	23:38	0.99 meters Low Tide
05–21	06:37	3.24 meters High Tide
05–21	13:04	1.35 meters Low Tide
05–21	18:58	2.80 meters High Tide
05–22	01:10	1.03 meters Low Tide
05–22	07:43	3.31 meters High Tide
05–22	14:11	1.04 meters Low Tide
05–22	20:16	3.12 meters High Tide

05–23	02:29	0.96 meters Low Tide
05–23	08:38	3.39 meters High Tide
05–23	15:05	0.70 meters Low Tide
05–23	21:17	3.46 meters High Tide

She begins paying more attention to who is on the table. Although it still pains her to look at their faces, she forces herself to do so while they are anywhere in that room. She remembers distinguishing marks on their bodies, a name that perhaps escapes from one of the nurses' mouths, sneaks a glimpse at the patient's chart. When she places the fetus in the garbage, she pays attention to which of the bins she puts it in, the blue one or the brown one. She locks away all of the information, repeats it to herself as she walks back to her room, writes it down in a little notepad she keeps under the floor mat. The same as she does with the tide tables.

When she sneaks out at night, she is more anxious than when she first began swimming across the channel. A much bigger risk. But after what happened to Mrs. Matsu and her nearly full-term baby boy, she doesn't care; she will never forgive them for that, never forgive them for making her a partner in it. This is what pushes her, late at night, to go behind the clinic to the garbage bins. When she first started doing this several months back, she got some oil from Mr. Shirayama's tool chest and lubricated the lids of the metal garbage bins so they wouldn't creak. Now she only has to remember the color of the bin that she threw the fetus in.

On this night, she goes to the blue one, lifts the lid,

pulls out the bag that she placed in the far right front corner so it wouldn't be totally immersed in the day's other garbage. She cradles the bag under her left arm while closing the lid, then hurries off to the northeast end of the island. Once she is away from the clinic, she takes a breath. She didn't realize in those early days of doing this that she was holding her breath much of the time when retrieving the bag. Now she is keenly aware of it, and she keeps the breath within her for a little bit farther each night that she does this. Maybe, on this night, only a step farther, three steps. I could make it the whole way across the channel on one breath, she thinks to herself, which brings a smile to her face.

Mr. Matsu is there to meet her, as she knew he would be. This as much his idea, his passion, as it is hers. Certainly much more personal. She hands him the bag and leaves quickly. It is not unusual for him sometimes to be there late at night, but for her it is. On the way past the small shack where Mr. Oyama paints the urns, she ties a single green ribbon around the door handle and goes back to her room.

She feels nearly as alive as she did on those nights when she swam, the nights when she left the soap for the children. She goes over to Mrs. Matsu's futon and touches her on the left shoulder, where she knows she still has some feeling, tells her it is okay, that it is done.

The next day at work is long, longer because of the waiting, the wondering if it all worked out okay. When the clinic closes, she hurries across and down to where the gardens are, where Mr. Shirayama has his little work shed. She turns over the wheelbarrow, leaves it upright, picks up the small cloth sack with the urn in it. On her way up to Building A-7, she hides the sack among several large rocks. This evening, it is quite easy finding the woman—Mrs. Wakano—for she saw the nurse holding the chart yesterday morning before the procedure. Saw the name, even the building number. All she has to do is go there and ask for her.

A-7 is no different from A-10, where she lives, or any of the other dozens of buildings for the patients. She enters the building and takes a deep breath. This is the most difficult part for her.

"Where can I find Mrs. Wakano?" she asks the first person she sees.

"Straight down the hall, the second wing on the right."

"Thank you."

She goes to where the woman told her and immediately picks out Mrs. Wakano from the other patients in the room.

"Mrs. Wakano?"

She wonders if the woman recognizes her from the day before but imagines not, for she had on her mask.

"Yes."

"I'm Miss Fuji from A-10. May I speak with you for a minute?"

"Yes."

She stands there, hating this moment when fear rushes over the patient's face. With some of them, the look disappears as quickly as it came; with others, it sits there heavily, impossible to move. She waits a few seconds before realizing that Mrs. Wakano thinks that she meant in the room, not in private.

"I'm sorry, but outside, if it's not too much trouble."

They walk down the hall, saying nothing. She wants to talk to her, reassure her that everything is okay, but she knows that she mustn't say anything in order to protect both of them. When outside, Mrs. Wakano speaks first.

"What is it you want?" Her voice is guarded.

"I'm here to help, Mrs. Wakano. I was in the clinic yesterday."

They continue on without talking, passing a cluster of patients.

"I have been assigned to Clinic B for the past few years and—"

"I know who you are, Miss Fuji. I remember you were the one swimming at night. It's okay."

"Thank you, Mrs. Wakano." She feels uncomfortable that instead of she consoling Mrs. Wakano, Mrs. Wakano is consoling her. This isn't the first time that this has happened, but she hasn't gotten used to it, may never get used to it. They walk up the small path and she removes the cloth sack from behind the rocks.

"This is for you. I know it isn't much, but it is all we can do."

Mrs. Wakano opens the sack, pulls out the blank white urn. She says nothing.

"I can't keep it."

"If you don't want the ashes, we understand. Some

people have scattered them in the sea, others around here; some don't want them at all."

"No, I want them, for both my husband and me, but it's too much of a risk. I don't want any more problems, Miss Fuji."

"We know. We have started a shrine over there on that small island. Tomorrow night, there will be low tide at about eleven-thirty. We can cross over, and then you can go there with your husband anytime and visit."

Mrs. Wakano closes the cloth sack, hands it back to her.

"Thank you, Miss Fuji. I will meet you back here tomorrow night at eleven-thirty."

She crosses over to Key of the Hand Island with Mr. Shirayama and Mrs. and Mr. Wakano. The late-May night is cool, the first night of the quarter moon; each of them has a small kerosene lantern to help them cross. When they climb the ninety-five steps and arrive at the top, she unlocks the small shrine that they have built while Mr. Shirayama holds her lantern. Mrs. Wakano grips the sack while her husband pulls the urn from it. They step to the shrine and place it inside, where the other sixteen same blank white urns rest. They light a stick of incense and a candle, then say a prayer. She and Mr. Shirayama pick up their lanterns and leave Mrs. and Mr. Wakano alone, telling them only that they must go back across the path before one o'clock, when the tide will close for at least another twelve hours.

ARTIFACT Number 0735
A Nagashima wedding certificate

"Miss Fuji, I have to ask a big favor of you," says Miss Min one night while receiving her massage.

"If I can help, I will try. What is it?"

"I shouldn't be asking you to do something like this."

"What is it, Miss Min?"

"It's embarrassing to ask."

"Please, just ask me."

"I want to get married and I need your help."

Her hands stop where they are, on Miss Min's lower back.

"I'm sorry, Miss Fuji, I knew that I shouldn't have put you in this position."

She smiles and her hands get moving again.

"I would be glad to try to help you. I'm just shocked that anyone would ask me to do such a thing."

"It's Mr. Munakani."

"The one with leprosy?"

Miss Min, stunned, looks back at her. And they look at each other for quite a while before they both start laughing. They laugh and laugh, so loudly that others passing by can hear. She takes her hands from Miss Min's back to wipe away the tears, using her sleeves to avoid the ointment on her hands. Then, after a calm in the laughing, they both start up again, and more tears run down Miss Fuji's cheeks. This keeps up until she finally sees Miss Min through a watery blur, and she realizes that there are no tears in Miss Min's eyes, or on her cheeks, or on the futon.

Where do all those tears go? she asks herself.

"I would be glad to help you, Miss Min," she says once again, removing the towel from her back and helping her on with her cotton robe, which she sleeps in.

"Thank you, Miss Fuji."

"It's okay."

"No. Thank you for the laughter."

"You, too, Miss Min. Good night."

"Good night, Miss Fuji."

She closes the door, arrives at her building, feeling alone. When did the tears of laughter turn to such a river of sadness? She knows that tonight will be one of little sleep.

The following week, she goes to see Mr. Munakani. Miss Min and Mr. Munakani have known each other for quite a while. He is a former naval officer and has an interest in Korea, often talking to Miss Min and a few other of the Koreans about their country. She often feels a sadness when around Mr. Munakani because he still has enough of himself left from before the disease for her to see what he once was. Still hints of broad shoulders, strong hands, a tough, square face, large eyes. With some of the patients, it takes some imagination for her to re-create them, and some she can't do at all, but with Mr. Munakani, it is easy.

She feels uncomfortable with this position of go-between, not sure about how to bring up the subject. The past few nights, she has gone over and over possible ways of approaching it:

Miss Min would like to marry you.

What do you think about marrying Miss Min?

I know someone who would like to marry you.

All seemed too direct, childish. She wanted to go and ask someone for advice but thought this would be wrong. She knows nothing of this task of go-between, nothing of the formalities.

They sit drinking barley tea, sharing small talk and rice crackers. Then it is out there.

"Miss Min would like to marry you, Mr. Munakani."

It shocks and relieves her at the same time. The longer Mr. Munakani doesn't say a word, the more difficult, awkward it is. She wonders what she did wrong. Was there something she skipped?

"I can't, Miss Fuji. I can't ever allow myself to marry."

"She's a wonderful person."

"That she is. But it's not Miss Min I object to. It's not that at all."

She sits there, not sure where to go next, so she allows Mr. Munakani to speak when he is ready. She wishes she had more barley tea to drink.

"It is the rules of this place that stand in the way."

"Rules? You are allowed to marry, Mr. Munakani."

"Yes, I know. But if I get married, I must agree to sterilization. And that, Miss Fuji, I can't do. Not even for Miss Min, who, as you say, is a wonderful woman. They may take everything else from me, but this is one thing, at least for now, that I have control over."

She thinks of how she will tell Miss Min. But what is there to say?

"At the clinic I've heard the doctors tell patients that in a couple of years after the sterilization, they can be desterilized."

"You believe too much of what they say, Miss Fuji."

She holds the teacup in her hand, stares into its emptiness, a few granules of brown tea at the bottom.

"Who has ever heard of such a place? A place without the playing and laughter of children."

She says nothing, again waits for him to continue if he wants.

ARTIFACT Number 1059
     A medical release form

"Of course you can leave, Miss Fuji," Administrator Kaneko says.

She stands there before his desk, stunned at the words. Even more startling to her than the fact that she is even standing there. Something she went and did, no real plan, just walked right in and asked to speak to him. Is it possible that if she had asked five, ten years ago that the answer would have been the same? She wasn't prepared in any way for these words, so matter-of-fact. He digs through a filing cabinet and pulls out a thin yellow folder, tosses it on the desk while shutting the cabinet drawer with his other hand. He opens a folder, pulls out a paper, turns it so she can read it.

"We have patients go over to Honshu almost every day. However, in order for release, permanent release, Miss Fuji, there are a couple of rules that must be followed. First, you must be free of the disease for twelve months.

So, of course, that means the earliest you could get your release, if your test proves you are free of the disease, would be around this time next year. Secondly, you must have a job secured before you are given your release."

"A job?"

"Yes. We can't have you thrown out there without a way to support yourself. We don't want you to be dependent on others, troublesome."

"How can I get a job?"

"Now, I didn't say it was easy to do this. There are many other hurdles to overcome, Miss Fuji. You have to live near a sanatorium so that you can get your medicine each day."

"Can I go back to my diving?"

"Sure, if you return each day and get your medicine."

She thinks of the rowboat that brought her here. Impossible to return each day.

"Can't I be given a month of doses at a time? Or go to a clinic?"

"We can't do that. The laws don't allow the distribution of the medicine other than single doses. Thus far, there have been no medical establishments set up to distribute medicine in the communities."

She pulls her eyes away from the paper sitting on the desk in front of her. The walls are blank except for a couple of medical certificates. She gives Administrator Kaneko a quick bow and turns to leave.

"But Miss Fuji, don't you want to take one of these release forms with you?"

"No thank you. I'll come back and get one at a later date."

Again, she gives a quick bow before opening the door and leaving the room.

ARTIFACT Number 1012
> From the bookshelves at Nagashima

When you are lonely and have nothing to do,
Let this song be your friend,
In place of I who hardly come to you.

> —Empress Sadako's tanka for Hansen's disease patients

Unless I illuminate myself
like a deep-sea fish
Nowhere would I find even a glimmer of light.

> —patient, Akashi Kaijin, from the
> tanka collection *Haku Byo,* 1939

1. Leprosy is a disease like tuberculosis and other infective diseases, and is not a result of a curse.
2. It is not a hereditary disease.
3. It is caused by small germs similar to the germs of TB.
4. There are two types of patients, the infective and non-infective.
5. It is only the infective patients that spread the disease to others by contact. Out of about 1,500,000 cases in India, only about 400,000 are infective.
6. Leprosy is curable, and in recent years there have been great advances in the treatment of this disease.

7. Leprosy is preventable. All necessary
   precautions should be taken for protection
   against infection.
8. In addition to the rational and helpful attitude
   on the part of individuals, an organized and
   determined effort on the part of the whole
   community is required to eradicate leprosy.

—from *Leprosy in India,* by Dharmendra (1958)

Among the discussion topics at the 1958 Global Leprosy Conference are: the organization of leprosy control programs in the South-East Asia and Western
Pacific Regions and the latest findings on Promin and
the disease and the policy of isolation. The disease,
medical experts state, is rarely contagious and they call
for an end to quarantine of most patients.

—from the 1958 Global Leprosy Conference;
host city: Tokyo, Japan

ARTIFACT Number 0199
Woman, sixty-one, painted on an urn

Less than twenty miles away, in the city of Okayama, the
streets are lined with flag-waving citizens as the runner
carrying the Olympic torch passes by. Miss Fuji is walking
back from Clinic B when she passes Mr. Oyama, and he
greets her on this January evening.

"One thousand eight hundred and seventy-one."

ARTIFACT Number 1609
A wheelchair

She isn't sure what to make of the rain. It hasn't rained here before on any of her birthdays, and today she is forty-three and doesn't know what to think. As she has on every birthday since her uncle's visit, she goes down to the dock after sunset, but this year she takes an umbrella with her. It isn't a heavy rain, only a steady drizzle. One where, if she were going out for a quick walk, such as the half mile from her room to Clinic B, she wouldn't even take an umbrella, allowing the light rain to dew her face, her hair, her clothes.

It was in a rain much like this one, just months before, when out pushing a patient in a wheelchair, that she slowed her walk and stood there for a second, turning her face up to the sky, feeling the rain against it. She had remained like that for a little while before realizing that the patient was getting wet. She pushed the wheelchair quickly, almost breaking into a run, as if to make up for lost time, to hide her embarrassment. How could she forget, be so stupid, and before she could check herself, she had said what she was thinking.

"There's no reason to apologize. I feel things by re-membering them. I can still bring back the memory of the pain of a bee sting, how it is similar to that of a shot, but lasting longer. I remember leaving my umbrella at home in the morning, walking to school in the rain. A light rain, like today. I enjoyed it. My mother never understood why I did that, always told me that I was going to get sick. Maybe she was right."

"Right about what?"

"Me getting sick."

She slowed her pace a little, startled, looking at the patient pointing at himself.

"I'm joking, Miss Fuji."

She kept the wheelchair at a slow pace, but faster than when they had first started out from the clinic. Neither of them said anything until the patient told her to stop. By then, she had forgotten the rain and wanted to get the patient back to his room. Again, he told her to stop, and she did.

"Please, remind me how it feels."

She hesitated, wondering if he was joking, waited until he spoke again.

"Remind me."

She leaned her head back, as she had done a few minutes earlier, again allowing the drizzle to graze her face.

"It is a warm rain, and it falls so softly that it almost tickles as it hits my face. But as it gets very close to tickling me, to where I want to rub my face, the tickling stops, and it goes back to feeling warm and soft again."

"Thank you."

That day, she had felt good, almost excited, as she moved the wheelchair again, as if she had learned something new, had taken a step forward somehow. Maybe it was the simplicity of what had happened, but suddenly it all started to become clearer to her. How all those years here she couldn't understand how the patients could damage their hands and feet, how they could be so careless, how it angered her. How, even though she was surrounded by them, she was one herself—the longer she stayed here, the more she needed to remind herself of this—and maybe this made it all the more difficult; maybe it took something as simple as a light rain to make her understand them, and herself, a little more.

And, today, in the darkness of her forty-third birthday, it is the same kind of rain that falls as she stands on the dock holding an umbrella, which she has yet to open. She is early, as on every birthday, but there isn't that rising excitement there had been the previous years. Because of the rain. Not that it doesn't feel good, for it does, but because of the fire and whether or not he will climb to the top of the mountain and make one—the mountain for which she still has no name, not sure if she ever knew it or whether she has forgotten it. And what if he doesn't light the fire tonight? she thinks. What do I do then?

She isn't sure how long she has been waiting, whether the rain has picked up or if she has been standing there long enough for the rain to start getting her wet, uncomfortably so. She waits as long as she can and then opens the umbrella, the rain still soft enough that she must concentrate to hear it hit the umbrella, soft enough that it takes awhile before it gathers and begins dripping from the edges. Still, there is no fire on the mountain, which she can't see the outline of, but there have been other birthdays where she couldn't see its outline, and then magically the fire would pop out of its head, putting some shape back into the island for an hour and a half.

She tries counting the number of years she has come down here to the dock for her birthday and is shocked that she can't differentiate between the years, the birthdays, for nothing about them is different, unique enough to help her mark the passage of the day, the years. She knows that her uncle visited her in her fifth year here, and she does the math: nineteen years; she can't believe that today is the nineteenth year that she has been coming here. But it must be so, she tells herself; the numbers don't lie.

Would I still be diving? she begins to think, but she stops herself from those dangerous cliffs of a question. She backs away from it, but in doing so, she bumps into another troubling question: Is it because of the rain that there is no fire or because there is no one left to make it?

It is well past eight o'clock; she can feel it in her tiredness. She closes the umbrella, surprised to find that it is no longer raining, and returns to her building where this week she is the first on night watch.

The question accompanies her all through the next day, and it walks with her down to the dock that night, and it is still with her the following day and again down at the dock that night as she stares in the direction of Shodo Island. It remains dark, dark as the answer to that question: Was there no fire because of the rain, or was there no one left to make it?

ARTIFACT Number 2209
A star chart

On this late night, walking home from Clinic B, she hears
a somewhat familiar sound far above her, but one that she
has only heard during the daytime. She looks up and sees,
for the first time at night, a distant jet slicing through Cas
siopeia.

ARTIFACT Number 1625
A stalk of wheat

The mother is passing through the shopping area of Mushiage when she sees a group of people coming her way. She
has just come out of Kato's Noodle Shop, where she
bought some fresh buckwheat noodles for that night's dinner. There are five or six of them nearing. One appears normal; initially, she thinks it is a staff worker, but the closer
he comes, she sees he is not. They pass within several feet
of her. She doesn't move, holds her breath as they near.
One of them is being led by the elbow; he wears dark
glasses, and his nose is so deformed, flat almost, that the
glasses slip off his face, only to be saved from the ground
by the strap tied around the stems. When this happens, one
of the others places the glasses back on the man's face, until they fall again. As the man is about past her, the glasses
fall from his face, no one noticing, and there he is, his head
turned toward her. There are no eyes beneath where the
glasses were, no eyebrows, no eyelashes. But there also

aren't bottomless holes like she had imagined, but sockets, skin-colored. She thinks that she has stifled the scream but doesn't know for certain. It seems as though he is gazing at her for hours, but they continue up the street, disappearing into the noodle shop.

The following Tuesday, she doesn't go to the shop for buckwheat noodles, but, rather, to the market, where she picks out some tofu and rice noodles instead. Back home, while washing the dishes, there is a knock at the door.

"Satomi, please see who is there."

She hears her talking to someone, and in a few seconds her daughter comes into the kitchen and says it is Mrs. Kato.

"Mrs. Kato?" she asks, even though she knows who it is and probably what she wants.

"Come in and have some tea."

"No thank you, I must be getting home to prepare dinner."

"Are you sure?"

"Yes, thank you. I was checking to see if you were okay. You didn't come by today, and I can't remember the last time on a Tuesday when you didn't come in."

"Oh, I was really busy here."

She feels her daughter in the other room, listening in, and wants to tell her to get back to her studies, but she doesn't dare.

"I will always deliver to your house; you know that."

"Yes, Mrs. Kato, and thank you, but it just slipped my mind."

They stand in silence until she again offers the woman some tea.

"No thank you."

She steps into a pair of sandals, slides open the door, and leads Mrs. Kato out along the narrow walk. When Mrs. Kato closes the gate and is in between the beam thrown by two streetlights, where she can't see the other woman so clearly, she speaks. "It's because of those people, isn't it?"

"Yes. I'm sorry, Mrs. Kato."

She hears Mrs. Kato's sandals clip along the street and watches her as she reappears under the streetlight and then fades again when she is between two lights. She continues watching her fade, appear, fade again, until she turns the corner of the street.

ARTIFACT Number 1764
A notebook of Mr. Shikagawa's

Still, after more than two decades, this is the way it is. She can't ever seem to view him in the present, only the distant past, that first day here.

From the first, she had admired him, but always from a distance. He lives on the opposite side of the housing blocks, in A-1, on the south end of the island. Before, she almost never had to go over to this end of the island to give massages or clean up after the patients, and even now as a nurse, there is rarely the need to go. But this morning, one of the nurses tells her to go up to A-1 and A-2 to get some blood samples. With the patients growing older, abortions are a rarity; her days, in recent years, have been filled with more traditional nursing duties—blood work, giving shots, physical therapy. She walks through the long narrow corridor, past the descending numbers—2019, 2018, 2017—and stops outside the door of 2016. She hears a voice inside. Not words from a conversation, but one word, then a couple, then nothing, another word or a couple of them. Not sentences. She isn't certain of the last time she has seen him, probably at last year's autumn bazaar—she usually sees him there. She waits for a pause in his words before knocking.

"What?" the same voice she has been listening to answers gruffly.

"I'm here to do blood work, Mr. Shikagawa."

"Come in, come in." Again the gruff voice.

She slides the door open, and in the middle of the tatami room, on the floor at a small table, he sits.

"Miss Fuji," she says, announcing herself.

His tone of voice softens a little. "Come in, Miss Fuji."

"They have sent me to get some blood work."

"Why at this time? Always in the mornings, when I'm busy."

"I'm sorry, but this is the time they send me."

"Not you, Miss Fuji. It is always nice when they send you. They don't send you enough. Sit down and rest for a while."

"I have quite a few blood samples to do."

"That's okay. Only for a few minutes."

She sits across the table from him; between them is a notebook, single words written all over it. She reads a few of them: *clang, gong, ring, strike.*

"It's my writing. I'm sorry it's not so neat. The feeling is slipping away from my hands."

She slides back a little, surprised, although she knows that she shouldn't be, that he knows she was reading the words.

"It's okay to look, Miss Fuji. I don't mind. I'm trying to find the right word for a ringing bell. Maybe you can help me."

"I'm not much for words, Mr. Shikagawa," she says, thinking of deer drinking from the river.

"I don't believe that. Your name is quite beautiful, and that was all your doing."

"I should be getting your blood work."

"Which arm do you want?"

"Let me see."

He holds out both arms while she searches for a good vein.

"The right one today."

He lowers his left arm, keeps the right one out for her.

"May I ask you what you were doing when I came in?"

"Writing."

"I know, but what are you writing?" she asks as she withdraws the needle.

"Poetry. Tanka poetry. Do you like poetry, Miss Fuji?"

"I can't say that I have ever read any. I went a couple of times to the storytelling sessions. But that was a long time ago."

"Ever since Mr. Yamai died, they haven't been the same. He was a wonderful writer."

"He was a writer?"

"Yes. He wrote short stories. Had several of them published. The best writer on this island."

She looks at him, his face close to his notebook, the small flesh-colored craters hidden by the blue glasses. Mr. Shikagawa is one of the patients whom the medicine hasn't helped, one who has built up a resistance to the new drug dapsone. His condition over the past few years has deteriorated, first the nerve function in his eyes and now the lack of feeling coursing throughout his body.

"Can I ask you something, Mr. Shikagawa?"

"Of course, Miss Fuji."

"How do you know what you have written down in those notebooks?"

"Each night, one of my roommates reads to me what I have written down each day, and I remember it, add to it the next day. Sometimes it's only a word; it takes maybe a week or a month to find the right word."

"One word?"

"Words are the most important thing we have. A few words, one word, can change history. Imagine that the correct words had been chosen by those people who are in charge of our lives. A few well-thought-out words and things might have been different. Unfortunately, they have chosen all the wrong words."

ARTIFACT Number 1390

A packet of sunflower seeds

She crosses the channel for the first time during the day. It has taken weeks to convince her that it isn't so bad to go over there. Many years have passed since she went on those late nights, and still she has told no one. The patients believed, still do, that she was going for swims, not crossing the channel, not actually setting foot on the mainland.

It has been even more difficult to convince Mr. Shirayama of this day trip.

"There is nothing over there I care or need to see. It's not going to make my life any different."

Finally, she coaxed him.

"I'm going, so if I can, you can, as well. It's only for a few hours; it will be something different, be good to get away for even a little time," she says, repeating the speech given to her over the past weeks.

Now, they are all on the ferry, eight of them, and no one is talking, each somewhere in thought. Some of the patients are turned to the shore of the mainland, others to the shore they have left, she, caught in the middle, looking into the channel, at the trail of water left by the ferry. She can't believe how nervous she is. The ferry goes south, down the channel, past the dock to which she used to swim. They go about a quarter of a mile farther before the engine is cut and the ferry is guided to the dock, greeting it not with the thud she has braced herself for, but with a squeak as they hit and the current pushes the ferry up against the large tires tied to the sides of the dock. It has taken about six minutes more by ferry than for her to swim across.

They help one another down the ramp onto the cement dock. The captain of the ferry, a staff worker at Nagashima, tells them that the afternoon boat leaves at three o'clock and that if they are not there, they will have to swim back. She thinks that he means it as a joke, but she isn't sure.

This part of town is new to her, and for now she isn't too apprehensive. It isn't the unknown that makes her uneasy, but the known, the streets she roamed late at night, the small fishing dock, the man, the two children who are now grown and would never recognize her, nor she them. The autumn air is cool; the wind seems different over here, if only because it is coming from a different direction. Still, after all these years, she is surprised by her intense dislike for autumn, for what it represents, what it represented— the far-off diving season, the excruciating winter to follow. They continue on a small road, following near the channel, passing where the ferry had brought them.

"How are you doing, Mr. Shirayama?"

"I don't know why I let you talk me into doing this."

"Because they talked me into it."

They pass more houses, but she sees no people. She can't help but feel that they are being watched, sure that there are people watching or at least hiding behind a cement wall, or in a thicket of a garden, or in a house.

Although this is certainly not a daily occurrence for the patients, two others, like her and Mr. Shirayama, have never been here; the others come over a few times a year to buy some things—mainly seeds, gardening supplies, and fabric.

She pays close attention to where they are going but is still surprised to find that they have reached the main street, the one that leads straight up from the dock to where she used to swim. Looking to the right, she sees the dock, the channel, and, beyond it, Nagashima. If the water wasn't so rough, she could get a better glimpse of the dock where she spent so many hours of her life, the rocky shoreline. But today, the autumn breeze has stirred up the channel, and she remembers how on days like this she would have to stand on a rock or on the sandy hill if she didn't want to lose sight of the children in the jagged water.

She keeps looking, until one of the patients guides her away from the dock and up the street where she went that first night here, and on the other nights, as well. Now there are other people, not many, but some. She feels eyes, some staying on them a long time, following them, others fleeting. She peers right into the back of the head of one of the patients. She isn't sure whether she is breathing or holding her breath. They continue up the street, nearing the fish market; she can hear the voices from the stalls off through the small side streets. She wants to run in the opposite direction, down to the dock, swim as fast as she can over to Nagashima. They stop, and she asks Mr. Shirayama why they have done so.

"Mrs. Makibara went to try to buy some sunflower seeds."

They stand on the sidewalk and wait.

"We used to eat in that noodle shop there," a patient says, pointing to the building, its metal shutters pulled down, a sign—OUT OF BUSINESS—hanging on the front. "They had the best buckwheat-noodle soup."

She fears that she may make eye contact with someone, or maybe someone will be looking at her. Doubts as to whether she could survive over here shatter her. For so long she has felt that she could make it over here, on this side of the shore, but now it is daytime and all the people are out and she is no longer protected by the dark of night or the channel.

The farther they go, the more she resents them, not the people of this town but the seven patients with her, they, the source of her doubts today. How they coaxed her into this, how without them, she is certain, she could walk these streets unimpeded. She would only stand out as a stranger, a visitor, somehow connected to this town, not a freak. The word her sister used—*freaks*—and now she doesn't believe that she could defend them as she did on her sister's visit, doesn't honestly believe that she can do so. If she were alone, they would never know; she'd sit at a counter, eat a bowl of ramen or some sushi, and no one would think twice about serving her, would make small talk and she would be on her way.

One of the patients takes her by the arm, whether to urge her along or to be guided by her, she isn't sure. She smacks the arm, smacks it again when it doesn't move, realizes that the arm doesn't even know that she is smacking it. They pass the bus station, a thought rushing through her to run to the bus, go wherever it is going, as far as it is going, and then get on another bus or train or whatever and take that as far as it will go. On and on. Anywhere but here with them. The bus pulls out and away from the station and from them. A man in the back of the bus turns and looks out the window at them.

As they enter a small park, she begins to doubt that,

even if alone, without any of the patients, she could get served here in the shops, or board a bus, for she would know who she is and it would somehow spill out, telling everyone. And it is here that it is pounded into her that she is one of them as well, that she is no different, no matter how she may appear. The same. Over there, across the channel, the patients are dependent on her, but here she is as dependent on them as they are on her. Maybe more so. All of them are getting along much better over here than she. Mrs. Makibara has bought her sunflower seeds; they are all now placing the plastic sheets on the ground, getting ready to have the lunch that they have prepared. She is the only one sitting on the bench at the far side of the park, cold with sweat, feeling unsteady. At the opposite end of the park, a young woman is playing with a small group of children, all wearing the same uniforms and hats. She still has her eyes on them when Mr. Shirayama comes over and sits next to her.

"Are you okay, Miss Fuji?"

"I don't know. I feel a little dizzy."

"Try to eat something. This is difficult for all of us. Maybe it's too much being here for the first time."

"But I've been here before."

Mr. Shirayama's face is puzzled.

"This is where I came those nights. I didn't just go swimming; I used to walk these same streets. Only it was night and there was nobody out here. And I was alone, wasn't with any of you."

The severity of her words shames her, leaving Mr. Shirayama as if she has slapped him across the face. He stands and returns to the blanket that the other patients have laid out. He must have said something to them, because they eat for a while before one of the patients comes over with a couple of rice balls and a piece of fish.

"I'm not hungry."

"You should eat something; maybe it will make you feel better."

"I'm not hungry." She tries to be nice, wants to be polite, wants not to hurt them, but wants even more to be left alone, and she can't bring any warmth into her voice. The patient takes the food back to the blanket.

She notices the sun, the shadows it is casting, and figures that she must remain here another two hours before getting back to the ferry and returning home to Nagashima.

ARTIFACT Number 1139
A photo from the dock, looking
toward Shodo Island

For weeks, she has thought of this day. And now it is here and she is standing on the dock early, as on every year. This year, she needs no umbrella for the night is clear; it hasn't rained for more than two weeks. She has been standing here for more than a fist of the passing crescent moon. About an hour, she thinks, remembering one of the patients telling her that the length of a fist held up to the horizon is about an hour's distance for the moon to travel. The moon is now on her second fist and she knows the answer to the question that has trailed her since her last birthday: It wasn't because of the rain that there was no fire.

ARTIFACT Numbers 2027, 2028, 2029
A harmonica, an accordion, a drum

The first time she hears it, she thinks it is in a dream. Distant, but clear. Then she thinks that it is the wind whistling up from the Inland Sea and through the cedars, but she doesn't feel the wind. There are two different kinds of sounds: first, a high-pitched moaning, and later that is joined by a musical instrument—a harmonica perhaps. There is a pattern to them, a repetition, with breaks every fifteen or twenty seconds, and then it starts back up again. The more she listens, the more she is convinced that the second one she is hearing is a musical instrument, a harmonica. The first one, she can't place as any instrument she knows.

Still, she can't imagine where it is coming from. Maybe it is one of those nights when the wind is just right and sounds carry across the channel—the engine of a trawler, the bark of a dog, voices even, although she can never understand what they are saying, but certainly voices. She has tried to put faces to those voices—maybe the man on the fishing boat she had seen on her late-night swims, or maybe the boy and girl. But this thinking makes her weary, the faces always obstructed by night or distance.

Leaning up on her elbows, she checks to see if anyone

else is awake. They're not. Miss Kitanami is supposed to be on night watch, but she has fallen asleep against the wall. She wants to wake someone, ask them if they, too, hear it, see what they think it is. She tries concentrating as to which ear the music first enters, from the right or left, but she knows how sounds can play games. Maybe her hearing is fading, she thinks, perhaps from the diving, like—she pauses, takes a second to remember her name— Miyako; dear Miyako, how the air pressure had damaged her hearing, so many of the older divers' hearing. She has often imagined this happening, getting older, having to lean in closer to a conversation to hear it, closer each year, until she would be nearly on top of the person. How she would talk louder, thinking everyone else also had trouble hearing.

Her worries about her hearing are shoved away by the fact that she couldn't recall Miyako's name. Her mentor, her favorite of all the divers, the one who fed her while she hid in the horrible weeks before arriving here. She tries recalling the other divers' names and can only come up with five or six; she can recall some of their faces, their bodies in the showers, but not the names. Maybe it isn't her hearing that is fading, for the music is clear; maybe it is the repetitions of the days that are dulling her mind.

The second one is a harmonica, she tells herself again, almost certain that it is coming from the hill to the east of her room, up there near the suicide cliff. But why, and who? She wants to go outside and see, but she remains there listening to the music, wondering if someone on the other side of the channel is also awake, also listening.

For the third straight night, she hears the music. Tonight, there is a drum added to the harmonica and the other instrument. She has thought of asking others if they, too, have heard it, but she doesn't, allowing herself to enjoy the remote possibility that she is the only one who listens to it each night, a personal performance. Tonight, however, it is too much for her, and she steps into her sandals, walks out into the early March night, and follows the music.

The plum blossoms are late this year, and their white flowers, although dulled, can still be seen silhouetted against the cloudy night sky as she walks up the hill. She likes the plum blossoms more than the cherry, their beauty equal, she thinks, and the crowds are always smaller and she can enjoy them more. The slight grade up the path is rocky, although not as bad as it used to be. She has recently seen a few of the patients, with their large bamboo baskets, hauling rocks from the path, others raking and sweeping it. The difference is quite noticeable, and she imagines that someday she may even be able to walk the path in her bare feet.

The music gets louder the farther she goes, but then suddenly it stops, then picks up and starts again from the beginning. She has no idea of the song, but she recognizes the same notes played over and over again. Repeated about every half minute.

Rehearsal is the word that comes to mind. How things are done over and over until nearly perfect, and then over and over again. The repetition, almost like diving. How she could rate each and every day of diving, good or poor, or that rare near-perfect day when her lungs felt fresh each and every dive, her hands finding exactly what she wanted. Those rare days—maybe once or twice a season.

She is at the door of the large building atop the hill, the opposite side of which, only a hundred feet away, is the suicide cliff. She has never stood atop the cliff, night or day. Has seen it only from below. From down below, with the sea curling in and around the rocks, there's almost a strange beauty to it, but up here, although it is night and she can see very little, it is cold. Cold enough to make her forget the music coming from the building behind her.

She turns and almost runs over to the building, the music pulling her into it. Once again, she hears the music, that same twenty-second spurt of a piece or piece of a piece that she has heard for the past three nights. The sliding door is open; a lizard with a tail twice the length of its body sits on the door frame. The music has stopped as if on cue, as if they know she is there. She is to the side of them, a dozen men sitting on wooden chairs atop the tatami floor. Although the night is cold, some are barefoot. Several hold their harmonicas to their mouths, ready to play; others rest them on their laps, listening to the man sitting on a stool in front of a set of drums.

A hitting together of two wood blocks and the music starts up again. First, there is that sound that she couldn't place; it is coming from some strange instrument that a man holds, pulls open and closed, small piano keys on one side. A cumbersome-looking instrument. As he opens and closes it, she thinks of a giant handheld fan, opening and shrinking. The pace begins slowly and then the harmonicas join in, picking it up until it is almost frenetic, the drum boom, boom, booming in the background, pulling the pace gradually back down again until only a creaking of a chair is heard.

"You have to play together, all the same pitch. There are too many individual tones running in and out of here. Let's try it again from the beginning."

They do, that slow pace picking up, peaking, and then going back on down.

"Again."

She can't decide how the song makes her feel—good or desperate, or both, up and down, as with the music.

"Okay that's better," says the man at the drums, although she doesn't recognize anything so different from the previous times they played. "Let's take a break."

The man comes over to her, the drumsticks under his left arm.

"I hope we are not disturbing you."

"No. I heard the music for the past few nights and I was wondering where it was coming from."

"Let me introduce you to the Blue Bird Band. We are going to perform a concert here this summer. As you can hear, we need practice, but we have some good players."

"It's nice to hear music."

"Thank you. It gives us something to carry around with us during the day; we can practice in our heads, which helps to blank out things we don't want to think about."

"The only music I have heard here are several songs that I call up in my mind. But it seems that some days I can't do it. I forget them or I can't find them."

"I hope that this band will put some new songs in your head and that you can recall them anytime that you need."

"What's the big instrument?"

"That's an accordion. You've never heard one before?"

"No, I don't think so. Where did you get it?"

"Before I came here, I used to teach high school band. I've managed to get a few older instruments donated."

"I hope you continue on with it. It's nice."

"Come back and listen anytime you like. We'll be here almost every night."

ARTIFACT Number 0901
  A story told by Miss Min

While the urn—Woman, fifty-five—is being painted, she goes down to the bottom of the cliff. It has been awhile since she has been here. The winter has been long; she has fought a cold all through it, and today is the first time in several months that she has felt well enough to sacrifice the extra hour of sleep. As she walks through the darkness of five o'clock, she wishes she had stayed back on the futon. She feels as though she is a stranger to this part of Nagashima, would, on a normal day, be chilled by the thought that maybe she has lost another piece of this place, like the shore where she used to stand, years ago, across from Mushiage, like the dock from where she began and ended her swims. But, today, she knows she has lost much more than a piece of this island.

She steps along the shell-crunchy shore, heading over to the large rocks. Although the sun is not yet up, the sky has given enough light for her to see. Once she makes her way atop the third rock, the highest in the cluster, she feels a stranger here no more. It is the familiarity of these rocks that she likes most, how they never seem to change, how they take so long to be worn away by the sea, by the wind, the bodies that have hit them. The passing of time is so much kinder to them than to us, she thinks. She looks at her hands, which are as they have always been, short, thick-fingered, but now there are creases running around them and the skin is looser. And the rest of her body, not only her hands, is softening, too.

She sits on her favorite rock.

The sun is up, still hidden by the small hill on the eastern side of Nagashima. It is not a spectacular sunrise in any way, which lessens her guilt for not coming here more often.

She remembers the day when she first went over to Key of the Hand Island with Miss Min and wishes that she could go back and tell her of the bird she has seen, the fish that it has caught. Today, she thinks again, I have lost more than a piece of this island. While looking over at the path, which is still under the sea, she would like to pray, but that has never been something for her. So she thinks of a story that Miss Min told her one day while she was giving her a massage:

He watches his mother as they climb. She leads the way, whether making it easier or more difficult for him, he isn't sure. It is the middle of October, the beginning of autumn here in the central part of the country. The higher they climb, the closer to winter it becomes. Near the top, where they will stop, it will be two weeks closer to winter than down in the valley.

"I can watch the leaves change colors and together we can fall when it is time to rejoin the earth," she told him and his wife two days earlier. It was one of the rare mentions since making the decision the spring before.

Knowing that others have done the same, been doing so for awhile, doesn't help him, doesn't ease at all the raging, repeating, mocking question: What are you doing? He has heard about the son carrying his elderly mother or father on his back all the way up, but it is these words that propel him up the mountain. His mother, although seventy, needs no help; it is he who wants to stop and rest. He who wants to take the load off that question, peel it from his back, set it on the ground for a while.

Once again he is caught in the middle, wondering whether stopping will prolong the day's pain or whether it will become a moment he takes back and will perhaps, one day, savor. Stop right there and sit on that fallen tree, have a nice talk, just the two of them. But they keep on climbing; neither has said a word since they left the house two hours ago.

It was the previous spring, while out viewing the plum blossoms, when his mother spoke of it. She said that she knew how difficult it was to feed everyone with the small rice field, told them she didn't want to become a burden on them and that she wanted to do this. His wife turned and bowed deeply to his mother, showering her with praise for her thoughtfulness and courage.

"We can't do this," he whispered to his wife late that night on the futon.

"You heard her; it is what she wants to do. We are not forcing her."

"But it's my mother."

"It's her choice. It can't be helped."

She stops about three-quarters of the way up the mountain. She breathes heavily, but not much more than he.

"I stop here."

"I thought we were going to the top of the mountain."

"Here the leaves are still changing. On top there are few trees."

He looks away, not sure what to say, or how or where to place his eyes.

"You should go on before it gets too late and turns dark."

What do I say?

Where do I look?

What will be left of me after this?

"Go on."

He looks up from his lowered head. She's on her knees, bowing to him, like his wife does, will do at the entrance of the house when he returns tonight. He bows back to his mother; both look, but neither can hold it.

Before he realizes that he has done so, he has taken

the first few steps down the mountain. He imagines she is still on her knees in a bow, but he can't, doesn't dare, turn around, and knows that if he does, he won't be able to go through with it. Only when he has walked fifteen or twenty minutes does he look back. Just trees. The same ones he didn't notice an hour ago. He stops and looks a long time at the trees, this path, and he knows that he will never see them, will never walk this path again.

Weeks later, the man is certain that if only he knew for sure, the pain would subside.

One morning on the way to the charcoal factory, he sees, up above the mountain, distant crows and hawks soaring in a circle.

Two days later, he sees an old man walk by with his son and he wants to confront them, ask them where they are going. But he remains silent, pretending he doesn't see them heading toward the base of Mount Otake.

The following week, over by the shrine, he notices the maples, which are scalded red. The cedars remain dark green; what's left of the oaks, gold. All enhance each other. Here in the valley, when the colors are at their most vibrant, he knows that up in the mountain the leaves have already fallen.

ARTIFACT Numbers 2030, 2031
Two musical instruments

Other instruments, other songs have begun to enter her nights. Instruments she finds much more soothing than the accordion and harmonicas. Instruments that can ease her into sleep: a cello, a bass. Instruments she hears for the first time: maracas, a lute. Instruments she is familiar with: a Japanese *kodaiko* drum, a bass drum, tambourines. And now that she can differentiate between them, she allows herself to take in the music, some nights lying awake listening, some nights going up to the Lighthouse. A couple of times, she has even fallen asleep there, on the tatami mats, the rehearsal all around her.

ARTIFACT Number 2188
A homemade beeswax candle

At least for tonight, the patients will have names, she thinks. Their given names, if they know them; if not, the ones they chose in their first week here. She knows very few of the names, most before her time here.

They paint their Nagashima ancestors' names on thin *washi* paper cut into six-inch squares, four squares per lantern. Some work on the frames of the wooden lanterns, others making the candles from beeswax. The paper sides are attached to the frames, the candles secured inside. It takes the better part of a day and the following night on the final day of the August Obon holiday. They go down at dusk to the shore at the bottom of the cliff. The night is sultry, no hint of a breeze even down here on the shore; the mosquitoes are greedy. They wait until it is dark, stars bright, mixing in with the specks of light from Shodo Island. A soft orange glow in the distance on the mainland. First, she thinks it is the remnants of sunset, but when it doesn't go away, she realizes it is the lights from the city of Okayama, twenty miles away. They all have matches, and for those who can't strike them, the others do it. The matches pop and flare; the candles inside the lanterns are lighted, illuminating the names painted on them. Above them, atop the cliff, the pounding every few seconds of a large drum thunders over them.

She helps a couple of the patients launch their lanterns in the water and then gets the first of hers—Miss Matsue, December 1946, painted on the sides. Carefully, she sets it in the sea, the lantern for the patient she has never met, and it floats away along with the other lanterns, a crooked river of light crawling, illuminating the way home for the spirits.

She goes over and picks up the second of her lanterns, lights the candle. Next to her, Mr. Munakani, the former naval officer, is preparing the lantern for Miss Min. She waits for him, and they send them off together. On the sides of her lantern, the name of her uncle Jiro is painted, along with the years 1971 and 1972, the year when she last saw the fire atop the mountain on her birthday, and the year when she first didn't see it. She watches until the last of the lanterns burns out, or drowns in the sea, and only the echo of the drum is left behind.

ARTIFACT Number 2083
A small black-and-white television

On this March evening, she passes by Building C-7 and hears it. She hears it but can't believe it, stunned. Never before on Nagashima has she heard this. She imagines

things that sound like it: a bawling cat perhaps——there have
been a few over the years; the wind through the trees, but
she dismisses this almost immediately; one of the musicians
squeezing the likeness out of an instrument. It stops, but
then begins again. She looks through the window and sees
a gray glow, some patients and a couple of nurses watching
a TV as a mother changes the diaper of a screaming baby.
She stands there until her breath steams the window and
she is no longer able to see into the room.

ARTIFACT Number 2400
        A brochure of the Blue Bird Concert at
        Kyoto City Auditorium

Three days before leaving Nagashima for the second time,
Mr. Oyama gives her the key and she goes that evening. It
is still an hour before dusk, but inside the windowless oval-
shaped room, it is dark. She takes out the flashlight, goes
past the rows of white urns from left to right, finds the one
with Man, twenty-seven, on it, making certain that this is
it; there is one other painted the same, but it is much more
to the left, from the earlier years. She removes the urn,
places it in the bag she has brought, locks the door, and
goes back to the Lighthouse, where the Blue Bird Band is
practicing.

When Mr. Endoh, the director of the Blue Bird Band, asks
her, she wants to accept, but doesn't think she can do it.
Memories of that trip to Mushiage are still very much with

her; the doubts have singed her. "It would be for only two days," he says, "and since you are our biggest fan, we would like for you to come."

And in May, she is here in the city that she passed through on the train with her uncle all those years ago. Now I am forty-seven; thirty-eight years ago I was here, she thinks. She sits, on this late morning, in the darkness of the empty auditorium, listening to the rehearsal. The band seems so small up there, not because she is that far away—she sits only eight or nine rows back—but because she is used to seeing them play in the Lighthouse, a room a tenth the size of this stage. She hardly listens to the music, has heard it all every night, over and over, for the past few years. Her mind is on something else this early afternoon in the Kyoto City Auditorium, sinking into the soft chair that flips up when her weight isn't on it. The longer she sits here, the shorter her time is to do what she must do. Something she has been thinking of doing so much that she isn't aware that she is thinking of it.

And before she knows what she is doing, before she can talk herself into, or out of, it, before she can applaud herself, she is out the door of the auditorium and onto the street with all of them. All the people of this city, who in the next few minutes will know who and what she is, or none of them will know. Everyone or no one, that's the way it will be.

Outside of the auditorium, although it is an overcast day, she shades her eyes. This is when she realizes that she has left her hat on the seat. The hat she has been wearing her whole life, it seems. To keep the sun off. But today, she thinks, I am not one of them. I don't need a hat or anyone to help me or tell me who or what I am or what I need or don't. There are taxis lined up on the street, a half dozen of them.

Ever since she accepted Mr. Endoh's invitation, she has studied the maps of Kyoto. But now that she is here, she can't move. Here, in the exact place where her finger started every one of those imagined journeys in this city. Started all of them here, finished all of them here, because this was the one place on the map that she knew for certain she would be. The Kyoto City Auditorium. From here, her finger stepped across great distances in no time: from the Heian Shrine, to the Golden Pavilion, to the teahouses, to the center of the city, to the Philosopher's Walk.

Now that she is here, not only a finger on a piece of paper, but all of her, she isn't sure what to do or where to turn. Her first step is in the direction of the taxis, and after a few steps, she stops. She has never been in a car, much less a taxi. She moves a little closer and observes. A man goes up to the first taxi in line, taps on the window, and steps back from the door, which magically pops open. She observes. Some of the taxis sit with their back left doors opened; others don't. She waits for the next taxi and then gets in. The door closes as bafflingly as it has opened. The driver turns to her. She wants to get out, run back into the security of the soft seats and the darkness of the auditorium, the music around her. She doesn't know how.

"Where to?"

"What?"

"Where do you want to go?"

"The Philosopher's Walk." She blurts out the first place that comes to mind, although she had wanted to go first to the Heian Shrine.

The taxi pulls away from the auditorium, and in a few minutes the driver glances at her in the mirror, asking, "Which end of the walk do you want to start?"

"Excuse me?"

"Which end? The north or the south?"

"Whichever is closer."

She keeps her eyes on the little machine in the front by the driver, the numbers it clicks off—200 . . . 230 . . . 260 . . . 290. She clenches her small purse with the money she has saved over the years, and that which Mr. Shirayama gave to her before she left.

"Is this your first time here?"

"Yes."

"Where are you from?"

"Okayama."

"The Bizen area? My family and I went there last year. My wife loves Bizen pottery."

"I'm from the Oku area, not far from Bizen."

She wishes the driver would stop talking, but she also doesn't want him to stop. The more he talks, the more he may find out; but also, the more he talks, the more comfortable she becomes, because she isn't being noticed. Maybe she could belong, could get along out here. Alone. The taxi stops and the door pops open, again surprising her.

"Seven hundred and twenty yen."

She hesitates, then grabs the first amount of money she

finds, hands it to the driver. He gives her back the change, pushes the little machine in the front, and the 720 disappears.

"Enjoy your stay."

"Thank you."

She gets out of the taxi and it pulls away. There is a small canal, running in the opposite direction—the Philosopher's Walk. She had never heard of the place before Mr. Yamai mentioned it, when she went in for a fresh bandage and gauze on one of those mornings when her leg was infected. Maybe he was from this city; she isn't sure why they were talking of it, but he said, "If you ever go there, go to the Philosopher's Walk. Away from all the tourists and crowds. It is a place," he said—and she remembers the words exactly, not because they made sense to her, but because they didn't—"that smells of that most beautiful smell, the smell of thought."

And she stands there along the narrow canal lined with trees, taking a deep breath, and another, she smells nothing other than May trees, the flowers, the canal. He was always much too educated for her, with his intense passion for knowledge. Along the canal, there are not that many people. The ones who pass pay her no attention. She goes slowly, searching for the right place to do what she has come to do. After rounding the bend, she sees no people within sight. She removes the small velvet sack from her handbag, opens it, and begins scattering the ashes in the canal.

"At least some of you has returned home, Mr. Yamai," she whispers as the ashes float by. Some of them sink. A large orange-and-white carp opens its mouth, as if the ashes are food, then slips back under the water. She stands there until the last of the ashes are taken away by the slow-flowing water. She follows them. And she continues on until a small waterfall carries them down and under the water to unknown places, where she can no longer go.

By the time she reaches the end of the canal, she is thirsty. She is surprised by how tired she is. Maybe it is the vastness, the distance, she thinks. At Nagashima, she can walk its entire length and back, covering almost every part of the island in an hour, an hour and a half. But here, an hour's walk, and she has only walked the length of the canal. She could continue on the entire day and still be in this city.

She sees some people holding cups of drink; she looks around for a shop where they may have bought them. There are shops selling shirts and souvenirs, but she sees nowhere to buy a drink. She enters one of the shops, buys a map of the city, and asks, "Where are drinks sold?"

"Those machines over there." The young woman points behind her, and she turns her head and sees a machine.

"Thank you."

She stares at the machines, pictures of cups, different names written on them. As with the taxi, she waits for a demonstration of what to do. Finally, someone comes over, and she concentrates on the steps he takes—money in the hole, push a button, open the little door, take out the drink. She removes a coin from her purse, slides it into the machine, and it's gone. She then pushes the first button on the left, opens the sliding plastic door, pulls out the cup, and jumps back when the liquid splashes her hand. She stoops and looks into the machine, sees there is liquid spilling out from inside. She picks up the blue cup, which she has dropped, looks around to see if anyone is watching her—nobody seems to be—and takes out another coin, drops it into the machine. Again she listens to it drop, then pushes the same button, but this time she waits before opening the door, waits a long time, until the woman behind her tells her that it is done, to take the cup out. She removes the cup, spills a little on her hand.

The woman does all the steps at the machine with ease, a naturalness that makes her feel clumsy, ridiculous, but at the same time victorious. She takes a drink from the black liquid and nearly chokes on its sweetness, isn't sure that she can finish it. There is an empty bench and she sits on it, thinking about the drink in her hand and whether or not she wants to, or can, take another taste of it. Almost like that bitter black sugar she had once as a child. Something that one had to acquire a taste for, her father had told her. She goes over to the public bathroom, dumps the remainder of the drink into the sink, and throws the cup away.

From the maps she studied back at Nagashima, she knows that she isn't all that far from the Higashiyama district of the city and its old teahouses, streets and buildings from long ago. She opens the map she has bought, finds where she is, marks the place with her finger. Higashiyama is about half a finger's length away. She marks off the route where she has gone—it is about the same, perhaps a little less—and then decides to walk.

She sits on the tatami mats, her legs curled up under her, traditional-style. The woman in the beautiful navy blue kimono sets the tray with the thick green tea in the bowl and the sweet bean cakes in front of her. The shop is pristine, decorated simply but elegantly. Vases of all shapes, various kinds of flower arrangements, a shelf for displaying the tea bowls and cups. She feels rough, awkward. The tea is good, bitter, and the sweet bean cake is a nice balance to it.

"How do you like Kyoto?"

She is caught off guard by the fact that the woman knows that she is a visitor, although she thinks that it must be quite obvious.

"It's wonderful. I was at the Philosopher's Walk this morning."

"Oh, that's a beautiful place. I go there often, sometimes in the evenings. How long will you be here?"

"Only for two days. I have to get back to work."

"What is it that you do?"

"I'm a nurse at a rehabilitation clinic now. I used to be a pearl diver, until I had to stop."

"Are you from Shima Peninsula?"

"No, down in the Seto Inland Sea."

"Isn't it frightening, the diving?"

"Just the opposite. When you are at the bottom and there's no one else around, it's the most peaceful of things. A friend of mine once told me about the Philosopher's

Walk and how he loved the smell of thinking there. I didn't smell anything different there this morning, but I think I understand what he was saying. And that is the way diving is."

The woman excuses herself for a minute. She sits there drinking her tea, thinking with amazement at how in such a short time, she has begun to create a life for herself, a new story, a history. How easy it has been for her to talk to the woman. She can be or say whatever she wants, but she stays rather close to what she is, doesn't want to step too far out of herself.

With the woman over at the counter, talking to another customer, she finishes the last of her tea, eats the final bite of the cake. And she reaches into her left pocket and pulls out one of the coins, sets it on the lacquer tray that holds the empty tea bowl. She is sure that the woman will see the oval-shaped one-sen coin on the tray. The front: black, trimmed in gold, a hole in the middle, the amount, along with the *kanji* for Nagashima Leprosarium.

She stands up and puts on her shoes, slides the door open, thanks the woman, compliments her on the tea, and slides the door closed behind her.

She has arrived at the auditorium in time for the concert. Her seat is in the center section, on the aisle, five rows from the stage.

She says good evening to the two women sitting on her left, wants to talk to them, but the emcee has come onto the stage. It is difficult for her to sit and just listen; she has so much energy, is enthralled by it, how she talked the whole time in the taxi on the way back here. And at the Heian Shrine, she asked questions she already knew the answers to, but she just wanted to talk. She adjusts herself in the seat, bumps the arm of the woman next to her.

"I'm sorry," she says, apologizing.

"No problem." The woman smiles.

When the audience claps for the emcee, she follows their lead and does so, too. She listens as he speaks, but she is more curious about the people in front of her, beside her. There are more claps, and she does the same. The curtain is drawn, and there sit the members of the Blue Bird Band. Polite applause from the audience. As the band begins to play, she slides into daydreams of her morning and afternoon, and this is where she stays until the high-pitched voice of a woman snaps her back to the fifth row of the auditorium. She opens her program and sees that the woman onstage is a famous actress, all shy as the emcee talks to her, her voice a perfect high-pitched female voice. The two women sitting next to her laugh and smile at everything that the actress says, enraptured by her. So this is why they have come, she thinks. This is what dragged them here, this famous actress, not the Blue Bird Band.

She is grateful when the emcee is through talking with the actress and the curtains close. As she is about to stand and let the two ladies out, she sees Mr. Endoh coming toward her. She doesn't want to talk to him, knowing that if she is seen with him, everyone will know she is with the Blue Bird Band. He is there before the ladies can get by.

"Where were you at dinner?" he asks.

The ladies are trying to get past, but Mr. Endoh has blocked the row.

"Just out sight-seeing."

"What did you see?"

"Just the regular places—the Golden Pavilion, Heian Shrine, a teahouse."

"What do you think of the concert?"

"It's wonderful."

"Do you want to come backstage and meet Miss Sugijima?"

"No. No thank you. Maybe after the concert."

"Okay, Miss Fuji. See you after the show."

She can now step into the aisle and let the two women out.

"Excuse us. Could you watch our programs?"

"Of course," she answers, looking over to their seats, where the programs are balanced on the armrests.

The second half of the concert is a blur. She knows that she never had to stand up to allow the two ladies back into their seats.

The concert is well past finished, the janitors are sweeping the stage, and the ladies' programs still sit on the armrests.

She is back at Nagashima, as if it never happened. As if she had never gone, had imagined it all, only another practice session in the Lighthouse, as if she dreamed everything. But there is one thing that continuously reminds her that she actually did go to Kyoto—the confidence of knowing she

could survive off the island. She knows her survival would
depend on only one thing: that she go out there alone. She
knows this, and she carries this knowledge with her for the
next decade and a half.

There are other trips for the Blue Bird Band: Nagoya, Osaka,
Tokyo, Kanazawa, Okayama. Although Mr. Endoh asks her
each time, she politely refuses, and as of late, those night
practice sessions, she rarely hears them, even when the
wind is blowing in from the southeast.

ARTIFACT Number 1446
A dried chrysanthemum

The daughter, Satomi, now finished with nursing school,
shares her mother's passion for gardening. Together, they
have started a small flower garden in the front of their
house in Mushiage.

They go into town to the vendor with the best flowers,
Mr. Satoh. The daughter loves chrysanthemums, and Mr.
Satoh has some beautiful ones this autumn.

"For the past few years, these have won many prizes,"
he tells them.

Although they are clearly more beautiful than the others, the price for them is the same. They buy two of each
color and take them home, placing them in the front of the
house, along the narrow path leading to the door, so that
anyone who comes to visit can see them. The whites and

purples and yellows are vibrant and the girl finds herself, for long periods of time, standing there losing herself in their beauty. So it is with great disappointment that she sees, only three days after she has bought them, they have already begun to wilt. She waters them that third morning, tries propping them up with some thin metal poles, but by the next morning they are dead. The next day, Satomi bundles them up and takes them back to Mr. Satoh. He offers to replace them, but the ones he picks out are not as beautiful as the ones they had had.

"I'd like those, like the ones I had," Satomi says.

"These are beautiful, as well."

"Not as much as those."

"But these will last twice as long."

"Why?"

He doesn't answer, busies himself with wrapping the flowers, turning his attention to another customer, who has bought some potatoes and mountain vegetables. When the other customer leaves, Mr. Satoh draws himself close as he hands her the flowers.

"There is no charge, of course," he says.

"Thank you."

He must sense her continued disappointment, so he draws close once again and says in a hushed voice, "You and your mother have been good customers, so I can trust that you will not tell anyone. Those flowers you bought the other day came from over there." He points toward the channel.

At first, she doesn't register what he has said, thinking

that his pointing means the island of Shikoku, some twenty miles away. Then, looking at his face, she can tell that he doesn't mean Shikoku, but Nagashima.

"Nagashima?"

"Yes."

"Why do you buy from there?"

"As you see, they are the most beautiful flowers. But"— he lowers his voice as a customer comes near—"you see, we have to spray them with disinfectant before selling them over here, and that is probably why they die so quickly."

She holds the new batch of chrysanthemums close to her, and Mr. Satoh moves away, places a few cucumbers and tomatoes in a bag, and hands them to her.

"These are service."

"Thank you."

Satomi takes the flowers home and, as Mr. Satoh said, they live much longer.

ARTIFACT Number 2388
A daily treatment schedule

Some days, she never steps foot inside the clinic other than to pick up and drop off a copy of the patients' charts. She can't recall the last time she has spent a week of days only in the clinic. Can't recall the last time an abortion was performed—she remembers who it was, Miss Inaka, but isn't certain when it was.

The only day that changes in her routine is the first of the month. The charts in each of the buildings that she is in charge of hang in the storage room, where the medicine is also kept. She loads her cart, on the top shelf of which she sets the medicines, together with a chart:

Multibacillary (adult dosage):

A. Monthly Treatment: Day 1
Rifampicine, 600 mg
Clofazimine, 300 mg
Dapsone, 100 mg

B. Daily Treatment: Days 2–28
Clofazimine, 50 mg
Dapsone, 100 mg

Duration of Treatment: 12 or 24 months.

On the bottom shelf of the cart, she places the medicines and a chart:

Paucibacillary (adult dosage):

A. Monthly Treatment: Day 1
Rifampicine, 600 mg
Dapsone, 100 mg

B. Daily Treatment: Days 2–28
Dapsone, 100 mg

Duration of Treatment: 6 months.

Her mornings are spent in Buildings A-4 and A-3, afternoons in A-2 and A-1.

As late in the afternoon as possible, she backtracks in Building A-1 from Room 2048 and goes to Room 2016, which, if she had followed the correct order on the chart, should have been visited at around 2:20 instead of nearly 3:30. She knocks and a voice answers.

"Come in, Miss Fuji."

Mr. Shikagawa is sitting on the floor at the small table, the cassette player and several tapes atop it.

"Good afternoon, Mr. Shikagawa."

"I told you that you don't have to knock."

"I know that you tell me that every day, but I will continue to knock."

"You're a stubborn person, Miss Fuji."

"As are you."

Mr. Shikagawa hits the base of his palms together and laughs, then bends over the table to shut off the tape recorder. No matter how often she sees this—it's been over a year that she has been coming here nearly every day—she watches as if seeing it for the first time. And she does so now.

His wrists brace the sides of the cassette player, his mangled hands jutting out at forty-five-degree angles, elbows on the table. He leans over, drawing his mouth closer to the cassette player, sticks out his tongue, runs the tip of it over the buttons—play, fast forward, reverse, record— pauses when he gets to the stop button, presses the tip of his tongue against it, shutting off the recorder. The clicking sound, although she knows it is going to happen, causes her to jump.

She has always prided herself on not showing pity or

feeling sorrow for the patients, but with Mr. Shikagawa, she can't help feeling, every afternoon when she sees this, a range of emotions from amazement to pride to sorrow.

"There isn't that much to do today, only the one tape," he says. "Today was one of those mostly thinking days. Some people call them 'wasting time' days, but they are necessary, maybe the most necessary."

"You don't have to explain all that, Mr. Shikagawa. I remember my mother telling me that I was lazy, that all I did was some diving in the morning. She didn't understand. She never knew what it took to be a diver, as I don't understand things about writing."

She goes over to the small closet and takes out the typewriter, sets it on the table next to the cassette player. After wiping the saliva from the player, she presses the rewind button and listens to it hum, thinking how incredible these machines are, how a person's voice can be on this thin tape. Just thinking about how it is possible makes her anxious.

She presses the play button. There are some noises, which she knows are Mr. Shikagawa moving around, getting settled. She has become aware of the different noises when he is changing his sitting position, taking a drink. When he is taking a longer pause or a rest, she hears him moving closer to the machine, hears his breath as he searches with his tongue for the button to shut off the cassette player. Those are abrupt. Today, there is only one side of a sixty-minute tape. Some days there are two tapes, but, as he said, today has been a thinking day.

The first words she hears are *clang, bang, din, boom,*

chime, peal, toll. She types them, then rewinds the tape a little to make sure she has transcribed them correctly. There is about a minute of silence, then the words *reverberate* and *gong.* He repeats the word *reverberate,* then again, *reverberate.*

"Please type the words *echo* and *duplicate.*"

She adds both of them to the list, knowing that this is how he searches for the right word, that the tanka is for the most part written, that he is playing with the combination of syllables and sounds and emotion that all fit tightly, perfectly into the thirty-one syllable poem, the five-seven-five-seven-seven line pattern. There is another group of words: *parabolic, elliptical, half-moon, bowl, umbrella.* She repeats this pattern of turning on and off the cassette player, typing, rewinding, repeats it until she comes to her name being spoken and she knows that she has reached the end of today's work.

"Come in, Miss Fuji."

"Good afternoon, Mr. Shikagawa."

"I told you that you don't have to knock."

"I know that you tell me that every day, but I will continue to knock."

"You're a stubborn person, Miss Fuji."

"As are you."

And then she hears the sound of Mr. Shikagawa sliding across the floor and the abrupt click as he shuts off the cassette player.

As the tape is rewinding, Mr. Shikagawa asks her to please read the words she has typed.

"Clang, bang, din, boom, chime, peal, toll, reverberate, gong, echo, duplicate."

"Cross out all of them except for *peal, reverberate, echo, duplicate.*"

She reads over the list a couple of times, and by the time she is finished, she has crossed out well over half of the words. He seems satisfied, slaps the base of his palms together several times. Now she knows for certain that he is happy with his day.

"That's wonderful, Miss Fuji. Thank you for your help."

"You're welcome. Is there anything else you need?"

"No thank you. I'm going to rest for a while before dinner. I'll see you tomorrow."

"Okay, Mr. Shikagawa."

She stands up and places the typewriter in the closet, moves the small table with the cassette player into the far corner, where Mr. Shikagawa will not fall over them. She writes the date on the tape, places it in the plastic box, and puts it on the far right side of the shelf, which is packed with more than a year's worth of cassettes, more than a year's worth of words.

ARTIFACT Number 1454
           A letter

She holds the letter, which was sitting on the table next to Mr. Shikagawa's cassette player.

"It's from Tokyo; the seal of the Imperial Palace is on the back."

"I sent them a poem of mine for the New Year's tanka contest."

"Should I open it?"

"Unless it's in braille, I can't do much with it."

She opens it carefully, preserving the seal. The letter is brief. She looks at it again.

"Are you going to read it to me?"

"Yes, I'm sorry."

She isn't sure where to begin—with the positive or the negative.

"Tell me the worst part first; then I'll know what follows will be no worse."

"It says that you can't go to the Imperial Palace because of your disease. You would be dependent on the help of someone and you can't present yourself that way in front of the Emperor."

"So that means that the good part is that they selected my poem."

"Yes, they did."

Mr. Shikagawa smacks his palms together.

"Aren't you angry?"

"Why should I be?"

"For refusing you the chance to go."

"My work has been selected; it's been recognized. That's what matters, Miss Fuji. My words have meant something to somebody."

"But they should be shared with the rest of the country."

"That isn't necessary. We know."

She can't let it go. Most of the night, she sits working on a letter, wishing that Mr. Yamai were here now or Miss Min, how they were so comfortable with words. They would have the letter done in no time.

It is three nights before she finishes and another few days before she gathers the courage to send it off. She never expects a response and she doesn't get one. So she writes another one, like the first, and this time she doesn't wait a week to send it off, but does so that same day. And she sends off a letter each week, so that by the end of the month, she has sent five. Silence.

She is propping up the tomato plants in the gardens near the administration building when she sees him walk out. Before she has time to talk herself out of it, she has approached him, her work gloves removed, and speaks.

"Hello, I am a patient here. May I have a moment of your time?"

"Sure. I'm Mr. Takamura; I represent the Eleventh District." He takes out a business card from his pocket and presents it to her.

She tells him of the letters she has sent off and what happened to Mr. Shikagawa, all the time hoping that no one in the offices will see her speaking to him. He listens, nods a few times, inhales deeply.

"I'm not so sure I can do anything about that."

"That's what I thought. But I thought that if this were corrected, or at least checked into, there would be many of us over here who would think very favorably of you. And now, of course, we have once again been given the right to vote."

He looks at her a second, then quickly to the Inland Sea behind him. When he turns around and asks her for her name, she knows that she has struck that seam of opportunity in him.

Four days later, she receives two registered letters. The first is from the Imperial Palace, written by the Emperor's assistant, who is in charge of the New Year's tanka contest. He apologizes profusely, saying they have received none of her letters and that there must have been some sort of miscommunication about Mr. Shikagawa's poem. The letter says that since Mr. Shikagawa is disabled and cannot present himself properly in front of the Emperor, he cannot be invited to the Imperial Palace, but someone would be most welcome to come and read his poem for him.

The second registered letter is a note.

"I'm glad that I could be of some help to all of you."

The note is signed "Representative Takamura."

ARTIFACT Number 3002
        A speakerphone

Mr. Shikagawa tells her the numbers and she presses each of the ten of them. She pushes the speaker button, places the phone back on the hook, and they listen to the rings. One. Two. Halfway through the third, a soft "Hello" comes out of the speaker.

"Hello, Kiku?" Mr. Shikagawa responds, fidgeting; his nervousness has him moving all over the floor.

"Hello? Who is this?"

"Masahiro," he says. This is the first time she's ever

heard his real name. He has always refused to tell her what his name was prior to coming here. And now she hears it, but she isn't sure that the person on the other end can understand him; she remembers how it was also difficult for her and how she had to concentrate on what he was saying to understand, to follow the conversation.

Without thinking, she moves close to the speaker-phone and talks.

"Kiku, this is Miss Fuji from Nagashima Leprosarium. Your brother is calling to tell you that his poem has been chosen to be read at the Imperial Palace on New Year's."

Then a loud drone comes out of the speaker, and she looks around, wondering what she did, how she disconnected the phone. She sees Mr. Shikagawa move back away from the phone, sliding his body across the floor, bumping into a table, which he doesn't feel. The phone drones, and she tries to find the button to shut it off. After pressing two or three of them, she finds the correct one and the droning stops.

ARTIFACT Number 1132
A photo of the building of the bridge

Nearly every day, they go, and there is talk of it. She listens, once in a while asking a question to feign interest, but she never goes. And for the next two and a half years, as the six-hundred-foot bridge connecting Nagashima to the mainland is being built, she only knows of it but never sees it. Doesn't ever see it because the only place on the island from where one can see the bridge is the rocky piece of shore that juts out into the channel, where she used to go and wave to the children.

She doesn't ever remember Mr. Shirayama being so passionate, so excited about something.

"Don't you see, Miss Fuji? This is a sign that we are gaining some acceptance, some understanding from the outside."

"You said that when the Blue Bird Band went and played their concerts. That was how long ago? But what does it matter to you? You don't ever want to go out there."

"It's a victory; they are all small victories. That's what's important, Miss Fuji."

"We are all getting much too old for small victories. Besides, a bridge isn't going to change people's minds about us. With or without this bridge, it is going to be the same."

"A small step forward is better than one back."

Until this autumn day, he has remained positive about the bridge and what it could mean. But when she sees him, she knows something has pierced his spirit.

"What happened, Mr. Shirayama?"

His eyes are on the Inland Sea and she knows where he is looking. The pathway to Key of the Hand Island is open and they cross it, but they don't climb the steps to where the small shrine and the urns of the unborn are, but simply sit on the steps under the giant *torii* gate, and this is where he tells her.

"Officials from the Ministry of Health have decided to put up a barrier across the road on our side of the bridge. They will begin construction on it this week. None of this was in the original plans. Everything was going so well, Miss Fuji."

"Don't let them do it."

"They have already decided. The official said that the barrier is there to help protect the patients. He said that the island is a place where patients get treatment and that people and cars have no business here and should not be let in. But isn't that what the bridge is all about, Miss Fuji, to bring us together, for a free exchange with society? A barrier is no better than the channel. Why are they even building the bridge? Is it only for show?"

She wants to shout at him. But she sits there and stares at the pathway they have crossed and how it leads to Nagashima and the dirt road that she has walked on thousands and thousands of times, and she knows that she will walk it thousands of times more in the coming years.

"Don't let them do it, Mr. Shirayama."

The western end of Nagashima is a steep seventy-foot climb through the pines and bamboo and then another gradual half mile up through a thick forest of trees. Several weeks before they begin cutting a road through this area, Mr. Shirayama and half a dozen other patients make their way up through here and they arrive at the bridge construction site wet and filthy. Their flashlights send beams bouncing off the land and to the channel waters below. Across the span, on the Mushiage side of the bridge, flashing red warning lights blink on and off. The silhouette of the giant crane looms over them. The gray arch-shaped bridge has been set in place a few weeks ago; below it, except for the large beams holding the arch in place, is nothing but the channel forty feet down.

There is the barrier, similar to one of those put up at a railroad crossing, a large pole that can be raised and lowered to allow cars through. Already it has been embedded in cement.

"I'm not sure how we are going to remove this thing. It is bigger than I thought," Mr. Shirayama says, bracing the flashlight under his arm, holding it on the barrier.

They stand without speaking.

"Well, we should get a little rest before the workers come," Mr. Shirayama says.

"Rest?"

"Yes. If we can't remove it, then they will have to remove us from it." Mr. Shirayama takes the roll of rope from around his shoulder, sets it on the ground, and sits atop it, bracing his back against one of the posts of the barrier. The others do the same, and they remain that way. Several have shut their eyes and are sleeping for the next couple of hours, and the first light of day seeps out of the Inland Sea.

At first, when he isn't in his room, she thinks that he is maybe over at Key of the Hand Island. But when she checks the tide schedule and sees that low tide isn't until later that evening, she goes down to his work shed and checks. He isn't there; the place is all organized, as if he hasn't been there today, but he has always kept it that way. She goes over a very short list of places that Mr. Shirayama might be at two o'clock in the afternoon. The only other places on that list are the gardens, where she is almost certain he isn't, because he told her that they picked everything last week, and the Lighthouse, which—since the Blue Bird Band stopped playing several years ago—has been turned into a storage facility for discarded things.

When she checks both of these places and still he is nowhere to be found, her concern grows. Her thoughts dart from Mr. Yamai to Mr. Nogami, how they were snatched away from this place for thinking and acting out on their thoughts, for trying to bend the rules, to break them; her connection to both men, and now to Mr. Shirayama, telling him not to let them build the barrier.

Not now, she tells herself, walking out of the Lighthouse and down the hill, passing Key of the Hand Island. They wouldn't dare do anything now, not with all the recent changes around here, the new look to the place.

Then she thinks of the bridge; maybe that is where he is. She hasn't been over there; she knows that some patients have gone and watched them work on it, but she has no desire to see the bridge.

She makes the steep climb at the western end of the island and continues the half mile through the thick forest. She is surprised, annoyed by how out of breath she is after such a short climb and walk. As she is about to look at the area where the bridge is being constructed, she wrenches her eyes away, looks down at the ground. She doesn't see, refuses to see what she has only heard about: the huge crane, the span of the bridge, which the men in the hard hats are working on.

Mr. Shirayama and the other patients have tied themselves to the posts of the barrier. Her initial reaction, although she knows what is happening, is to untie them, help them up.

"How are you feeling Mr. Shirayama?" She goes over to him.

"I feel surprisingly alive. I slept for a couple of hours like this."

"What's going to happen?"

"The patients' rights group up in Tokyo have been called. I think that we will win this one, Miss Fuji."

"Why are you so sure?"

"Do the construction workers look as if they care if there is a barrier or not? They only want to finish the bridge. It was the health officials who wanted this thing built here. Besides, I don't think any of the foremen want to get near us. When they do talk to us, it is from far away."

"Well, Mr. Shirayama, history is not on our side in these types of things."

"History is changing. Like I told you many times, Miss Fuji, one step at a time."

ARTIFACT Number 1497
              A speaker

It is as if, suddenly one morning, the voices are every-where. She recalls seeing over the past couple of months the poles being built all over the place, but she didn't think much of it, for recently, in the past year, many things have been changing here. The cement road and sidewalk she is on right now leaves her legs and lower back aching. She tries walking on the grass or dirt when she can, but there is so much of this cement and so little of the ground. Only if she goes all the way down past the gardens is there a good stretch of dirt. Even all the way down there, the voices follow her.

"Yesterday, the Tokyo Stock Market closed up forty-three points and the Nikkei Index was up six and a half points. Today's weather for the Kanto region will be mostly cloudy, with a high of fifty-seven. Kansai and west Japan will be mostly cloudy, with highs in the low sixties. There is a twenty percent chance of rain."

Every thirty feet, there is a speaker, and no matter where she goes, the words of the radio announcer from NHK trail her. Standing right next to a speaker, the voice is almost too loud for her. Then as she walks away from it, it fades, but as soon as she thinks that it will leave her alone, the next speaker starts to pick up in volume, until it also is too loud and the whole thing repeats itself. In any direction, there is always another speaker.

The deep voice of Mr. Enoyama, the young staff member at Nagashima, cuts into the music, which has started. "Good morning. Excuse me for interrupting, but I have a couple of announcements this morning. First, today's lunch menu will be miso soup, pickled radishes, red snapper, and rice. The specials at the Shopping Center are bananas, grapes, lemons, and eggplant. Don't forget that next Saturday afternoon from one to five there is our spring crafts show, held in front of the Shopping Center." In midsentence, the song comes back on and life outside of Nagashima continues, and it will continue until the speakers are turned off tonight at nine o'clock, when, once again, until tomorrow morning at six, the island will return to itself.

ARTIFACT Number 0908
A gallon of black paint

On each of the newly built whitewashed cement-block one-story apartment houses, the names of trees and flowers are painted on the upper right-hand corners: Pine, Forest, Bamboo, Evergreen, Chinaberry, Sweet Flag, Laurel, Dogwood, Chinese Parasol Tree, Iris. And the names of birds: Seagull, Spot-Bill Duck, Bulbul, Heron, Chick, Pheasant, Turtledove, Umbrella Bird, Canary, Robin, Bush Warbler, Quail, Mockingbird, Swallow, Goose, Falcon, Wagtail, Kingfisher, Java Sparrow.

ARTIFACT Number 1133
A photo of the ceremony for the
opening of the bridge

It is a sunny, pleasant May day, the humidity low, and the one-mile walk is nice. There is no steep climb through the bamboo and pines now; a paved road has been cut through all the way to their end of the bridge. She is surprised by the excitement that she feels, having for the past couple of years felt not much of anything for the bridge. But today it is here and everyone is going. Alongside her is Mr. Shirayama, and Mr. Shikagawa is being pushed in his wheelchair by a nurse.

When they arrive at the bridge, she stands there and listens as Mr. Shirayama tells Mr. Shikagawa about it.

"It is a gray half-moon shape, about sixty feet high, twenty-two feet wide, and six hundred feet long. From where we are, looking across, there is a small mountain, the channel is forty feet below, and off to the right are clusters of houses on the south side of Mushiage town. It's the most beautiful bridge."

She leaves both of them, passes the place where the barrier had been constructed, and walks out onto the bridge. Many patients, nurses, staff members, and some others in suits, whom she doesn't recognize, are gathered there talking. She goes off to the far side, rests her arms on the railing, and stares down into the channel, the water moving ever so slowly below her. It seems far, the channel below. Seems much farther than forty feet, she thinks. I used to dive nearly twice that depth and it took about a minute to get there, but from here, through air, with no water holding me back, it would take a few seconds to cover the same distance.

She tries recovering the excitement that she was feeling only minutes ago, and she walks along the bridge, away from Mr. Shirayama, not wanting to spoil this happiness that he has earned. That we have all earned, she thinks. But why don't I feel any of this joy that so many of the others are feeling, this victory? She continues on through the people, nodding, bowing to those she recognizes. She turns around and goes back toward the Nagashima end of the bridge, spots Mr. Shirayama in the middle of a crowd of people, and he is smiling. She crosses the end again unimpeded, where now not even the scar that was left after they tore down the barrier is visible.

The opening ceremony is just beginning as she leaves, taking the winding cement road down through the pines and bamboo, following it to where the Inland Sea can be seen.

ARTIFACT Number 2940
A copy of the Nagashima microbus schedule

She still likes to walk, but there are days when she doesn't have the energy, and on those days she sometimes rides the microbus.

WEEKDAYS: 9:00, 10:00, 11:00, 13:00, 14:00, 15:00, 16:00

WEEKENDS AND HOLIDAYS: 9:00, 10:30, 14:00, 16:00

Chiryto Health Center—Mutsumishita—Seibu Bathhouse—Hiiragi—Heisei Park—Enoki—Namihana Bathhouse—Oyama San-Cho—Shinso Auditorium—Lighthouse—Building C-7—Shopping Center—Fukushi Auditorium—Rosario Church—Akebono Apartment House—Building A-13—Nozomi Bathhouse—Hagi East Dormitory—Soyogo Dormitory

ARTIFACT Number 0954
A needle

Needles. An echo of her past. The sound of them against the whetstone, the three or four nurses scrapping the needles, a near-constant sound.

The doctors give explanations: blood, possibly sex, infected mother to a newborn, contaminated needles. No need for explanations. She has learned about hepatitis C from all her years as a nurse in Clinic B, the liver cancer or cirrhosis that most likely follows, how some of them fight it, how others slip quickly away.

More and more patients have become sick, and she is sick, too, and she knows it. She has been more tired as of late, not aging tired—she is not even sixty—but a much deeper, longer-lasting tiredness. She knows.

ARTIFACT Number 1858
An election poster

When she sees it, she can't believe it, and before she even reaches the pole, her anger has control of her. She tears the first one she sees off the pole without much problem, then rips it in half, leaving it behind on the ground. The next telephone pole is fifty feet away; she tears another off the pole, then in half, leaving it on the ground, as well. In the entrance of the apartment houses, the entrance of the cafeteria, the supermarket, at the bus stops. She knows that people are watching—staff, patients. No one comes to assist or stop her. But after a little while of doing this, she notices a couple of people with large garbage bags following not far behind, and they gather up the shredded posters and throw them in the bags.

ARTIFACT Number 2987
Man, seventy-one, number 3,425

Early this morning, she is down past the gardens. Mrs. Tsubame, in her electric wheelchair, gives her a good-morning bow. The July gardens are colorful—red and yellow peppers, onions, orange cucumbers, all almost ready for picking. One of the patients once told her that the orange cucumbers came all the way from Okinawa. She doesn't like them—they are too bitter for her—but she has always found them pretty.

On the other side of the island, atop the Hill of Light, the Bell of Blessing rings out six times. Before the echo of the final one has ceased, there is a crackle and then the speakers are on and begin their day; speakers that now she hardly even hears unless she wants to. She can walk the length of the island past every speaker and never hear a word of the baseball games that are played in the summer nights. She completely tunes them out. She recalls the night that she and Mr. Shirayama were coming from the bazaar and he was listening to his favorite baseball team—the Hanshin Tigers—play. At each speaker, he would slow down and listen to a pitch. How angry he was when, at exactly nine o'clock, the Nagashima staff worker's voice interrupted the game, said good night, and the speakers were silenced until the next morning at six. After that, she bought Mr. Shirayama a small radio so he wouldn't miss the end of his games.

The relaxed, familiar voice of the radio announcer from NHK starts in with the news, but the third story of the day is interrupted by Nagashima's announcer.

"Good morning. Last night, at one-oh-five, Mr. Naka-hara from the Seagull Building, Room seven oh oh eight, died of cancer. He was seventy-one years old. He was from Osaka. His religion was Shinshu. There will be a ceremony at nine A.M. today."

She listens to the announcement repeated. She tries to remember something about Mr. Nakahara, but she can't come up with anything distinguishing about him. He arrived a year or two before she did, was diagnosed with hepatitis C, developed liver cancer a year ago. Number 3,425, she thinks. An urn with "Man, seventy-one" will be painted today; his ashes will join the rest up in the shrine. She thinks of Mr. Yamai and how she spread some of his ashes in Kyoto. A strand of satisfaction slips through her.

The news comes back on in midsentence. She continues with her walk, past Mr. Shirayama's work shed, down along the rocky shore, anchors used on long-ago fishing trips are rusted, grass grown up, twisted all around them. There is something beautiful but sad in those anchors. She lowers the brim of her hat and keeps walking in the direction of the eastern hill, which the sun has cleared. The sun, although just beginning to stretch the shadows, is already hot. At the base of the hill, where the cement road has turned to dirt, stands the last of the poles holding the speakers. She walks away from the morning news, and when she rounds the curve, she is out of range of the voice.

There isn't much up on this hill; once in a while, on a clear day, she can see the cluster of islands in the Harima Sea, where once many fishermen from her island made their livings catching yellowtail, but she has heard that pollution has all but wiped out the trade. Today it is too hazy to see the islands. There is a rustling in the growth of weeds and wild grass, and she sees a long brown snake slither a few feet from her, moving across the path and into the weeds.

She looks over to Shodo Island, wonders whether the divers still dive or whether that area of the Inland Sea has also become too polluted. She thinks of the coins she buried among the olive trees every Saturday, can't remember how many she had buried in her four years of diving, but she knows where. The fifth row and the twelfth tree.

Her thoughts come back to Mr. Nakahara and the cancer that claimed him. Will this be my fate, too, after all these years fending off an ancient disease, only to be claimed by a modern one? Death doesn't frighten her; it never has, even when she was sixteen or seventeen, in her early days of diving. She remembers how some of the women got around the subject of death by telling stories, myths about how the Inland Sea claimed some of them. They were only trying to scare her, the young new diver, but she never believed what they were saying. One story was about how a diver once got her foot wedged between two rocks at the bottom of the sea and couldn't get loose; her skeleton could still be seen years later wiggling there, still clutching an oyster shell, a perfect pearl inside, but nobody dared to remove it. There was one about how a huge squid squeezed one of the divers to death. But the story she liked the most, maybe because she found it most believable, was the one where two divers fought over a large shell, wrestling for so long that they both ran out of air in their lungs well before they could resurface. The shell they died over sat in front of the shower rooms as a reminder to the divers. This story brings a smile to her face all these years after hearing it.

She heads back down the path, the sun becoming too much for her. Soon the faint voice over the speaker can be heard. She stops and braces herself against a dizzy spell. She waits it out and remains there for a few minutes. No, death doesn't frighten her; it's the numbers that do. What number will I be, 3,426? A nice round number, 3,500? It is almost like a countdown, she thinks. There are nearly six hundred of us left here now, and as the one number goes up, the other shrinks. Someday, not so very far off into the future, fifteen years maybe, the numbers will come to a stop—about four thousand on one end, zero on the other. Which of us will be the last? Soon nothing more than an old-age home.

She hears another announcement about Mr. Nakahara and the ceremony to be held for him. After a slight pause, the announcer rattles the papers and reads today's lunch menu, then the supermarket specials: tangerines, muskmelons, prunes.

She passes the speakers every thirty feet, and before she even makes it to Mr. Shirayama's shed, she knows that she will not be here to eat the soon-ripened vegetables. She knows that she must go. Knows that she can't let herself become a number here, an announcement woven through the lunch menu and specials at the supermarket.

ARTIFACT Number 001
   A box

The morning after she has left, Mr. Shirayama is riding by in his motorized wheelchair when he sees the box by the garbage bin, in front of the incinerator, near his shed. He picks it up, knows that it is hers. The lightness of it surprises him. Taking it up to the Lighthouse, he sets it among the other things in the building, which he, the week before, was asked to help organize.

He opens the box, which she has carelessly taped shut. He isn't sure why, but he believes that she wanted him to find it, let him decide what to do with the contents.

This is what he finds: some old Nagashima money and a worn one-yen coin; a red stone with a black stripe through it; several maps—a hand-drawn one of Key of the Hand Island, an old map of Honshu with tracings all the way from Okayama to Mount Fuji, a map of Mushiage; a tide schedule and a star chart; and a brochure from the Blue Bird Band Concert at Kyoto City Auditorium.

across

the

channel

Morning dawns later here, she thinks. Like she is in another country, rather than a two-hour train ride from Nagashima. Or maybe it is noon, or another night altogether, or thirty minutes since she has last left the bed. The curtains in the hotel, where she has spent the past four weeks, are so heavy, nothing penetrates them. At least not light; sound certainly does. The noise—car horns, gangs of young men on motorcycles riding up and down the streets, bus drivers announcing the stop, a bullet train rumbling by—she hears it all. She imagines she will get used to it; it also took her awhile to get used to the speakers at Nagashima.

The room is small, she has trouble sleeping in the bed, sheets stiff as slate. It is a single step from the edge of the bed to the wall, three steps from the bed to the bathroom, two from the side of the bed to the television sitting on the counter-table-desk.

She boils some water on the hot plate, makes green tea from a tea bag. The tea is bitter; she let the bag soak too long. She turns on the shower, lays a towel on the bottom of the tub, sits on it, allowing the water to bounce off her. When she stands, the water is too hot on her head, but down here on the floor of the tub, it is just right.

It is early when she takes the five flights down. She has used the elevator only once in her time here; she doesn't like that feeling of dropping. She hopes there is never a fire in this place, the stairs crammed with cleaning buckets, extra bath towels, boxes with small packets of shampoo and rinse, little soaps, discarded magazines, newspapers, comics. All the tiny things to keep the hotel going. She thinks of telling the night manager of the danger on the steps, but he isn't even there. At the front desk, she leaves her heavy key with the long plastic key chain with her room number and the hotel name printed on it—591 Intelligent Hotel. The night manager is standing outside by the emergency exit, and he bows good morning to her. He reminds her that breakfast is from 6:30 to 9:00 A.M. She walks down the street with nowhere in mind, but she is at the bus center within minutes.

All around, sections of the cement platform are wet. She looks for other signs of rain, doesn't remember hearing it last night. There is a splash near her and she sees a thin, scruffy man bent over, scattering water with the plastic bucket he carries. When there is just a little water left in the bucket, he flings the rest of it onto the cement, turning his body as he does in order to fan it out. He disappears into the bathroom and is back again with another bucket, repeating the same pattern. The man works his way through, in and around people hurrying by with briefcases in hand, cans of coffee, tossing lighted cigarettes onto the wet cement, others mashing them with their shoes, the last of the smoke streaming from noses as they jump onto a bus.

She stands in front of platform number 7, the chairs all taken, six of them by passengers waiting for a bus, the other two seats occupied by a briefcase and a girl's school-bag. All the time, she has her eyes on the man with the bucket, and when, in about five minutes, the next bus arrives, she claims an empty seat. Bucket after bucket, he must have more than one, she thinks, for he retrieves them too quickly. She watches him, notices a few others glance his way. It takes him about half an hour to finish the large platform, and by then she has a headache from all the noise and exhaust from the buses.

The man goes back into the bathroom, comes out with a small bag and a large set of pincers. He works his way around the platform, picking up pieces of paper, a can. When he finishes, a couple of discarded cigarette butts have already appeared. He goes into the room, returns again with the bag and pincers, gives the platform another quick going-over. When he finishes, he sits down next to a large black bag, a stack of newspapers tied with twine atop it. He removes his baseball cap, runs his hand through his dirty black hair, turns his head, and coughs deeply several times. He is younger than she first thought. He appears as though he hasn't shaved in weeks, but she has never been a good judge of this, still isn't, for at Nagashima nearly none of the male patients had any facial hair. He rests and she watches him as he enters the men's bathroom, where he stays awhile before coming out with his hair wet and combed back. Now, he looks even younger, perhaps forty or forty-five. His face is a little cleaner, but it is still unshaven, is even more gaunt. The man picks up his bag and the newspapers, goes up the escalator, and she can no longer see him, only hears his cough. She thinks of following him, but it is already past nine o'clock, and now she must go to the convenience store and buy herself something to eat, for she has missed breakfast at the hotel.

Each of the next two mornings, she sees the man cleaning the platform. It is on the third morning that she sits next to his black bag and waits for him to finish.

He sits down; the black bag separates them. Only as of late has she felt the need to speak; she is amazed that with all the thousands of people she passes each day, there is no one to talk to. She remembers when she was in Kyoto with the Blue Bird Band, how she had spoken to anyone who would respond. Her ravenous hunger to speak.

"How long have you worked here?"

He turns his head, peering over the top of the bag.

"I'm only cleaning up."

"Do you do this every day?"

"Clean?"

"Yes."

"Every day. I have been doing this about a year now, I imagine." He turns away and coughs.

"Do you like it?"

"Like it? I don't know if I like it. It makes me feel like I'm doing something."

"That's what I need."

"What's that?"

"I need to feel like I'm doing something."

"We all need that. What do you do?"

"I used to be a nurse. You should see a doctor about that cough of yours."

"You sound like a nurse. No doctor can help this cough. You worked in this city?"

"No, I'm only visiting. And you?"

"I came here a little while ago."

She catches sight of a clock, and again she has missed the hotel breakfast and feels hungry.

"I'm going to have some breakfast. Are you hungry?"

"No, but thank you. I have to be going back."

He picks up his bag and gives her a swift bow, then disappears up the escalator.

The man has finished washing up and is drying his face with a towel. He sits down, the black bag separating them, as it has for the past few days.

"Breakfast?"

She accepts the sweet bean roll.

"Do you want something to drink?" she asks.

"No thank you."

She stands and goes over to the drink machine behind

them. She inserts the coins, a fleeting memory of her time in Kyoto and how she pulled the cup out before the drink was poured. Now there are drinks in cans, little boxes, plastic bottles, machines all over the place. The first drink machine came to Nagashima a while back and they had one of the staff give a step-by-step demonstration on how to use it; she remembers how the rumbling of the dropping can startled several of the patients. She buys two little boxes of Chinese tea; they drop gently, hardly a sound. She hands one to the man. He bows and offers her another sweet bean roll; she declines, and he finishes it off, along with the tea.

"I'm sorry, I never asked your name. I'm Miss Fuji."

"I'm Yasu."

"Do you live near here?"

In the middle of a drink, he points over her shoulder; then when he swallows the tea, still pointing, he tells her.

"Over there by the river."

"That's nice over there."

He gives her a little twist of his head and nods.

"I've seen people fishing over there. Have you ever?"

"Sometimes, but there isn't much in the river except some sardines; every once in awhile there's a horse mackerel."

He wraps up the paper from the sweet bean rolls, takes her box of tea, picks up a candy wrapper, and throws them into the garbage.

"If people today had a little more pride, I wouldn't have to spend so much time cleaning up after them. But I guess as long as I'm willing to pick up after them, they will continue. See you tomorrow."

"Okay. Thank you for breakfast."

Afternoons, she spends roaming around through the arcade area and past, but rarely into, the department stores. The large department stores are so cramped, but sometimes she'll go in and sit on one of those benches they have near the bathrooms, let the air conditioning cool her. One day, while sitting, she saw a mob of people. She couldn't see why they were all pushing, and when she got up and went to have a look, she was shocked that it was a bunch of discounted umbrellas they were swarming over.

She thinks about going to the library, over there on the other side of the river. It is a nice library and she has been there a couple of times. At about two o'clock, she stands in front of one of the large department stores and waits, along with a small crowd gathering there. At exactly two, the large clock begins the melody and she sees the small dolls come out from behind the doors, two by two, twenty in all. Each is wearing a costume from a different place, a Japanese boy with a headband and small *taiko* drum; a girl with long black hair, wearing a hula skirt; another doll, this one with wooden clogs. At least once a day, she tries to come here and watch the clock, to see the children staring up at it, some dancing to the song. It is still a surprise to see so many children, any children. She watches the clock until all the dolls have gone back inside.

The crowd disperses, and when she, too, starts to walk

away, she takes only a few steps before stopping. She thinks at first that she is mistaken, but when she looks again, she knows that it is him. She isn't sure whether to say hello, but she quickly dismisses this thought, knowing how she would embarrass him. Besides, what would she say? Would she drop a few coins into his nearly empty hat? Like the dancing dolls, she retreats into the department store, trying to regroup her thoughts.

She is on the opposite side of the street from the department store, and if she doesn't see him, she will go over in front of the clock. Still, she hasn't figured out what to say to him, and ever since she first noticed him there, she hasn't shown up at the bus center in the mornings, choosing to eat her breakfast at the hotel. It is now nearing six and the clock will play only twice more today.

"What are you doing, Miss Fuji?"

Hearing her name startles her.

"I was looking for the time. How are you doing, Yasu?"

"I'm okay. I thought that maybe you had left town. I haven't seen you for a while."

"I went away for a couple of days."

"Where did you go?"

She doesn't have an answer and so pretends that she hasn't heard him.

"I saw you the other day watching the clock. Do you like it?"

"Yes, it is nice. I have never seen anything like that before."

"Why didn't you come over and say hello to me?"

"When?"

"The day when you were in front of the department store and you saw me."

Again, he leaves her without anything to say. She feels hot and takes out a hand towel, dabs at her face, the back of her neck. The traffic passes by; she hears the clock begin to sing.

"The clock is playing; you should go."

"I don't need to see it today."

She stands there, watching the shoppers, listening to the melody of the clock fade in and out of the noise of the traffic.

Late the next morning, she meets him at the bus center, as they had planned. There is somewhere he wants to take her, something he wants to show her. They ride the bus about twenty-five minutes from the station and are up near the base of the mountain. When they get off, she offers him some fruit.

"No thank you. I've eaten."

"You always say that you've eaten, but you're so skinny. Here, stick these in your pockets and eat them when you want."

Away from the bus stop they go.

"Where are we going?"

"I told you that I have something to show you."

They walk up the gradual slope of the road. The trees grow thicker; there are fewer houses. She buys them each a plastic bottle of juice from a vending machine. He stops every few minutes and they rest, take a drink of the juice.

"Why are you so fascinated with those drink machines?"

"I told you that they hardly have any where I come from. But they are everywhere, even up here near the mountain."

"Drink, cigarette machines. I heard that they even have them at Mount Fuji."

"Have you been to Mount Fuji?"

"No, only something I read about. Vending machines right on top of the mountain. Garbage all over. They say the stench along the trail is terrible."

She is silent, can't believe what he has said.

"Have you ever been there?"

"Many years ago. My uncle took me when I was nine. I don't remember garbage or any terrible smell."

"More respect for things in those days."

They continue up the road until they arrive at a small mountain trail.

"I don't think I can climb all the way to the top."

"Just a little more. What I want to show you is up this trail a little."

For another five minutes, they continue along the dirt path.

"Okay, they will be up along here."

"Who?"

"The men I am going to show you. You will see them scattered all through this area up to our left. Keep walking and I'll tell you about them later."

As he said, she sees several small clusters of men sitting on blankets or tarps; some of the men have on suits, others only a white dress shirt without a tie. One man is playing with a calculator; another has a comic book. A few are talking, while others are hunched over a mah-jongg board. After several minutes, they stop, having passed by about a dozen men. She takes a drink, tries to slow her breathing, dry the sweat that has formed on her face.

"What are they doing?"

"They come up here every day and stay until early evening, then head home."

"But what do they do?"

"They are living a lie, Miss Fuji. Each day, they leave home in their suits, take their briefcases, as if they are going to work. Their wives have even prepared lunch boxes for them. But what their wives don't know is that their husbands have all lost their jobs and that they come here and wait out the day before going home at night."

"Won't their wives find out?"

"Eventually, they will have to tell them or . . ." He pauses and takes a drink, adjusts his baseball cap. "Or they will find out. That's what happened to me. My wife found out. I didn't go up a mountain like these men; I went to parks or rode trains to different places. But I was living a lie, like them. Now I am just trying to live."

"You lost your job?"

"I became sick first; then I was released from my position."

"What's wrong?"

"I have a sickness, one they don't know much about. It's rather new. One that deprives a person of all dignity, one that leaves you to wither away, to die alone."

She stares at him, not to bore deep into his being, but

her years as a nurse have taught her to notice physical signs. Other than the cough and a blisterlike spot on the side of his neck and the one she has seen on the top of his forehead, along the hairline, she sees nothing else that would make her believe that he has leprosy. His thinness doesn't point to this, either. He stares back at her and she feels as if he knows something about her, as if he brought her here to make a point that she, too, is living a lie.

"So, you are not from around here?" she asks.

"No, about one hundred and fifty miles from here. My wife and son now live with her mother. They told her family and friends that my company transferred me to Tokyo. That's why they haven't seen me around. On the holidays, they say that I am too busy to come home, or they go away for the holidays, say they are meeting me and we are going to a hot spring or something."

"Don't people think that it is a little strange?"

"Maybe at first, but the longer it goes on, people let it go, just keep quiet about it, as if it will all go away."

She braces herself against a tree, takes a deep breath.

"Are you all right?"

"I'm sorry, but I have to be going back. I don't feel so good. It's probably the heat."

They retrace their steps along the path, passing the men, many of whom have opened their lunch boxes, taken out their chopsticks, and have begun eating.

Her restlessness won't allow her to sleep. Within seconds of leaving the hotel, she finds a taxi and takes it to the beginning of the arcade shopping street. It isn't as late as it seems, but the arcade is quiet now, only a few people out. A fast-food restaurant remains open. The rest of the businesses have their metal shutters pulled down; boxes of garbage are stacked in front.

This is a street she has walked often during these past two months, but it appears so different at night, without the crowds. From the corner of her right eye, she sees one of the boxes move. This is one thing that she feels best about herself—her eyes have always been sharp; not the disease or age—she is sixty-four now—has damaged them. She turns around, sees the boxes move again. Looking closer, she sees that they are not boxes of garbage, but boxes taped and strung together into a house. All along this street, under the roof of the arcade, there are these self-made houses.

The box houses are only on the right side of the street. She tries thinking of the significance of this but comes up with nothing. Not far from where she first noticed the moving box, a man, not all that much younger than she, stands and is running a plastic string through a couple of flat boxes. He slowly weaves the string through and around until it is one long sheet. Surrounding him, chest-high, boxes make a square. She wants to look down inside the box house, see what he has in there, but she doesn't go any closer than where she now stands. She moves her eyes to a cluster of men, who are wobbling and staggering against one another, laughing loudly, talking much too loudly for the distance between them. One of the men, a necktie hanging crookedly from his open collar, a gray suit coat on the hook of his finger, stops next to the man building the house and glances at him.

"What's that?" the man with the tie stammers, almost falling back, as if the words have shoved him.

The man continues working on the boxes, his head down.

"It's a box. No, excuse me, it's your house. Is that your house?" He laughs loudly; the other men with him jostle one another and laugh.

He repeats his question.

"Is that your house?" More laughs from the others.

She is so tired from this long day that she only wants to sit down right here in the arcade, curl up, and sleep. She leans against one of the shuttered shop doors and watches the drunk men laughing and taunting. The man still ignores them, stoops down and places the last flat piece of the box on top, works the corner strings through the top sides of the boxes. The roof shuts him in, away from the men. The drunk man knocks on the side of the box. Knocks again.

"Is anyone home?"

Before she knows what she is doing, she is next to the man, standing between him and his friends.

"Leave him alone," she shouts.

The man is startled, but he regains his composure, laughs at her.

"What's wrong with all of you?"

The group of men grow quiet; a couple of them try to muffle drunken laughs. One of the men goes over to his friend.

"Come on, let's go." He pulls him by the arm.

"Come on." He manages to get his friend to take a step, and the man's feet follow one step at a time. The others follow them down the arcade street; soon they are all gone and it is only their fading laughter that she can hear. She walks the opposite way, hears a soft "Thank you" come from inside of the box house. She doesn't answer, then turns left on a small side street and heads in the direction of the river, only two blocks away.

The river is a calm one, one that you can't see flowing until something floats by. She doesn't have to wait long before a bottle comes into view and meanders past. She crosses the bridge and walks along the narrow sidewalk. Shortly, she arrives near the freeway underpass. Cars rumble above; trucks seem as if they are dropping on her.

Here, there are more substantial houses, made of boxes, blue tarps, sheets of plywood, old rugs. A permanence to them. Outside, a woman is squatting, stirring a pot of something. They nod to each other. A small dog whimpers and roams as far as its chain permits. The houses, built close to one another, go on for about a hundred yards. She notices that many of them have small rugs or mats in front, a pair of shoes or slippers sitting atop them. She goes over the shoes, tries remembering what kind Yasu wears. They all look like his, yet none of them do. She isn't sure what to do or in front of which house to place the bottle of cough medicine she has brought.

A truck thunders overhead and she wonders how can they sleep with all the noise, the highway less than sixty feet above. She remembers those sleepless nights in her early months at Nagashima, and all the others that came, and she once wondered if she would ever sleep in her life again, but she did, and so, too, do they.

In this narrow hotel room, she knows she will not spend another night here. This hotel room, she thinks, where one can pull the heavy dark curtains tight, deceive the day by turning it into night, but where night is always itself.

This thought gets her off the bed and she throws open the curtains and the sunlight hurts her eyes. She takes a shower, dresses, packs her little suitcase, stands in line at the train station, and gets a ticket for where she is going, where she knows that her story must end.

Even before she arrives here at Shima Peninsula, a place she has always wanted to go, the most famous place in the country for pearl divers, she knows what she is going to do and how she's going to do it. There wasn't much of a choice. The what she knew before even leaving the station; the how came later while she slept on the long train ride on her way here. When she awoke, she was happy, knew that it was right. There will be no more controlling her; this time she will have the final say.

That she never gave any thought of returning to Shodo Island doesn't surprise her; she long ago lost any sentiment to go back to her home island for a visit. Maybe thirty years ago, but not now. It is the diving that, after all this time, still has a place in her life, the one thing that has never abandoned her. And this is why she is standing at the front desk of the hotel, asking about boat rentals.

"Yes, we have small pedal boats that you can rent for a thousand yen per hour."

"No, I don't want a pedal boat. Do you have rowboats?"

"Rowboats? Excuse me a minute, ma'am." The young man goes over to the woman at the other end of the counter and they talk. He returns with the woman, who asks, "Are you sure you want a rowboat, ma'am?"

"Yes, that's what I asked for."

"Who is this for, ma'am?"

"Me, of course."

"Well, rowboats are not something we usually get requests for. We have kayaks."

"Will one of these kayaks take me out there into the sea? Out where the divers dive?"

"Sure. Have you ever been in a kayak?"

"No, but I'm sure I can handle it."

"Kayaks are two thousand yen per hour. Would you like one?"

"Yes, but for tomorrow."

"What time?"

"What time do the divers go out?"

"There are three shows each day—eleven, one-thirty, and four."

"Shows?"

"Pearl diving, ma'am. We offer a ten percent discount on tickets if you're staying at the hotel. Also, if you're interested, there is a Pearl Diver Parade of Fire, where the divers swim out into the ocean with burning torches, and later the Pearl Diver Queen Contest."

She waits awhile before talking to the lady behind the counter.

"I'll just take the room for tonight. I'll check on one of the boats later today."

The room is twice as large as the small place she had for the past couple of months. She opens the curtain of her seventh-floor window and sees the blue sea. The woman at the desk confused her with all the talk about shows and parades. She probably thought that she was a regular tourist coming to see one of the attractions.

She takes the sidewalk down to the shore, hoping to get a glimpse of the divers. She doesn't see any, and when she asks where they dive, she is told she can find them over by the small pavilion. She passes quite a few shops selling pearls; she thinks of the pearls she had found in her years of diving— nineteen of them, about halfway to a full necklace. She remembers the one diver, the lucky one, who spoke so loudly, and how she was always finding pearls. The shops have shell necklaces, photo postcards of sexy-looking divers in revealing suits. She imagines herself in one of those partially see-through suits and laughs. How ridiculous.

When she arrives at the pavilion, there is a line of people, and she passes them. One woman tells her that tickets for the show can be bought over there by the restaurant. Again, this talk of a show. She buys a ticket, and when the gate is opened, she finds a seat in the pavilion, which is built out on the rocks and into the sea. She thinks of the vending machines that Yasu told her were atop Mount Fuji.

The show begins with a young lady explaining the history of the divers on Shima Peninsula. The young women, who are posing as divers, go underwater. There is a loud applause as the divers rise to the top, each holding up a shell, giving a beautiful smile and wave. She wants to tell the people next to her that in four diving seasons, she found nineteen, that those sexy suits are not what the divers wore, and that she, so tired from the dive, couldn't smile and wave. She excuses herself, leaves the pavilion, and finds a bench to sit on. The extreme weakness is upon her again, and while sitting, she looks around for a place to eat, but although she has hardly eaten anything in the past couple of days, she has no desire for food.

Soon it will be over. Soon she can give herself back to the sea. Her place. One final dive. Last night on the train, she had a fleeting sense of giving up, quitting; the guilt slashed through her. But she knows that it is only a matter of time, months, maybe a year. She is not ready for another fight.

She is too late for the Pearl Divers' Parade of Fire, but in time to see the last of the Queen Contest. Onstage, there are eight young women all wearing the same thin white semitransparent suits, divers' goggles resting atop their heads, and high heels. A man with a tuxedo and microphone walks up to each of them, asking the common questions.

"How old are you?"

"Twenty."

"What is your blood type?"

"AB."

He goes along the row of girls, asking the same kinds of questions. She laughs to herself, knowing that not a one of those beautiful, thin girls could last a single dive; they couldn't make it fifteen feet under before fear would thrust them back to the surface. Their little bodies couldn't stand five seconds of the cold. This isn't who we are, who we were, she thinks.

Late that night, as she sits in the outdoor stone hot spring, she can't even enjoy this, her final night here, the idea of which, only twenty-four hours before, she was so at peace with. A peace now splintered by her confusion over the day's events. She thinks how the final dive, which she had so much craved, has been crushed by the need to get away from this place.

A couple of women enter the hot spring and sit across from her, talking. One of the women goes underwater for a second and resurfaces.

"Look, a pearl!" She holds up the imaginary pearl in her hand. They both giggle.

Miss Fuji is exhausted, but she manages to stand up to leave, and as she moves past them through the waist-high water, she turns and says, "That's not how it was."

There is no dock where the taxi drops her off in Mushiage, only water. The wall where the dock was connected is nothing more than ragged chunks of cement. She stands and stares into the water, but it offers nothing to keep her interest. She picks up her suitcase and continues toward the fishing boats. A man stands on the prow of one, hosing down the outside of it.

"Excuse me."

"Yes." He turns around, still spraying the boat.

"Where's the ferry?"

"The Nagashima ferry?"

"Yes."

"Why do you need the ferry when there's the bridge?"

She doesn't know how to answer him, knows that he is pointing at it, but she keeps her eyes on the fishing boats.

"You have family over there?"

Again, she isn't sure how to answer him. But he has already walked away.

She leaves her suitcase on the dock, near the fishing boats, and walks into town. It has never been much of a town, just the simple main street, which has changed hardly at all. There is still the market area, with the same seafood smell as before, the place where there used to be a good noodle shop, now a parking lot, the bus station across the street. She enters a convenience store, picks out a couple of rice balls—one salmon, the other pickled plum—and a bottle of green tea. When the girl at the register tells her the total and puts it in a bag, she realizes that she has left her money in the suitcase.

"I'm sorry, I forgot my money. I'll be right back."

She hurries out of the shop, feels that everyone is watching her. Keeping her head down, she doesn't lift it until she hears the water against the dock, and it is this which reminds her of how close she is to Nagashima. How good it will be to see Mr. Shirayama once again.

Untying a fishing boat is easier than she had imagined. Instead of coiling the rope inside the boat, she leaves it on the dock. No need for a rope where she is going. Much of the town is eating dinner now; the fishermen will not be coming out to their boats for another few hours.

She ignores the small motor, pulls out the oars, points the boat eastward. The bridge is off to her left. Facing straight ahead, she rows; her suitcase falls against the side of the boat, and she leaves it there. She begins to turn the boat in a northerly direction. Now, she can look freely in two directions and not see the bridge. There are many stars out tonight, stars that she has missed; the city lights swallow most of them. It is the stars that keep her attention until the boat scrapes the rocky bottom and comes to rest on the shore.

epilogue

There are times, while walking here in the morning or going back home at night, that I think of how so many of the patients began their isolation in my town. The dock where the ferry used to take them across the channel was less than half a mile from where I grew up, from where I still live today.

Since I am one of the newer nurses—I've been here for less than two years—I have many duties. Some of them are medical-related, but there are many times when I have to do things outside of the medical realm. For the past couple of months I have spent a lot of my time up in the building they call the Lighthouse, along with Mr. Shirayama, sorting through all these items.

We haven't thrown out all that much, mostly pushing things around, the towering ceiling echoing each grunt and groan. Some of them are quite large—old desks, cabinets, shelves—and those we have left where they stand, until we can get some of the staff to help move them. But many things in there are small, tiny as a hand, a nail of a finger, even. And it is some of those that we are setting aside, things that cannot be parted with.

Everything is sorted into categories—medical, patients, entertainment, historical, miscellaneous—and by periods of time—prewar, the forties and fifties, the sixties and seventies, and the most recent times, from the eighties up until now.

There is a story for each thing in here—many of the things have multiple stories—sometimes bringing back a moment so vividly that Mr. Shirayama is lost for an unknown amount of time, sitting there, holding the item, remembering. For a while, I say nothing, then break him from his thoughts, ask him to tell me about it. There are times when it takes no more than a minute; others, half the morning. When he is finished, we set the item aside, categorize it, and move on to the next.

I remember a staff member taking me around the place when I first came here as a nurse and I kept thinking, it isn't as bad as I had thought. There were TVs, gardens, flowers along the cement pathways; the patients had electric wheelchairs, nice clean rooms; there was a small supermarket. And this is how I continued thinking about the place for my first two or three months working here. It wasn't until I was out on a walk with Miss Fuji that my thoughts started changing. We had stopped down at the dock and were admiring Key of the Hand Island and the Inland Sea, which was calm as glass. My hands rested on the handles of her wheelchair. We stood that way for quite a while before she spoke.

"If you didn't know what was behind you, this would be a beautiful place."

That is when I began looking at this place differently, began asking myself, What was this place like all those years when none of us were paying any attention? I started noticing those old ivy-smothered buildings that remained, the rotting boats, the old sheds, noticing what was underneath all the gloss, as Miss Fuji calls it.

Nearly every moment that I am with her, I want to tell Miss Fuji who I am, but as of yet, I haven't, haven't quite found the courage to do so. Sometimes, I feel that she senses it, but maybe that is only me. I'm certain that someday I will tell her, probably one of those things I will blurt out before I can stop myself from saying it.

This hot September morning, I help Miss Fuji with her sponge bath and her clothes. She doesn't want to eat much; she never eats much in the mornings. While she eats the peaches I have readied for her, I put away the futon, move the table back into the center of the room, open the curtains.

Although it is hot, a nice breeze comes up from the Inland Sea every once in awhile. Today, Miss Fuji wants to go to the Hill of Light and see the flower gardens planted around the large bell. I push her up the hill, for she refuses to get one of those electric wheelchairs. It isn't all that steep and there is a sidewalk winding its way up. A sweat has broken out on my face and I wipe it off with a small hand towel. I go and sit on the middle of the three steps leading to the platform where the bell is. The chrysanthemums envelope the platform, and, like the ones I used to buy so many years ago, they are still the most beautiful flowers I have ever seen. Miss Fuji gets out of the wheelchair and starts up the steps. I stand to help her, but she gently swats my hand away.

She pulls back on the wooden pole hanging from two large chains and throws it at the bell, sending a loud rumble all over the place. She does it again and looks over at me.

"Your turn."

I step up to the bell and throw the wooden pole, its rumble echoes, and I feel its vibration throughout my body. When I can feel it no more, I do it again.

Miss Fuji is standing there watching me.

"Can you hear the bell over in Mushiage?"

"Yes."

We say nothing else. She starts down the steps; this time she lets me take her hand.

Sometimes when the sun is warm and the channel still, I take my lunch down along the shore to the small inlet that faces Mushiage. There are times when I sit and eat my lunch while watching the channel, other times when I re-move my shoes and socks and wade out knee-high into the water. And it is from there that I imagine that I see two small children, my brother and myself, over there on the mainland, playing on the shore, answering the waves of a pearl diver with waves of their own.

acknowledgments

The following sources were of invaluable help in writing this novel: Fukuoka University Medical Library; Bethany Leigh Grenald's online article on the pearl divers in Japan; the World Health Organization's archives; the Leprosy Mission's website; Minoru Yasuhara's wonderful photos of Nagashima; the HIH Prince Takamatsu Memorial Museum of Hansen's Disease; and the book *Leprosy in Theory and Practice,* by Drs. R. G. Cochrane and T. Frank Davey (John Wright & Sons, Ltd.).

I'd like to thank the following in Japan for their help and support on this novel: the Nagashima Leprosarium, for allowing me to roam the island; all the patients at Nagashima, in particular, Mr. Tanigawa and Mr. Usami, for their incredible courage and for sharing their lives with me; Mrs. Ikenaga and Mr. Shimura, patients at the Kumamoto Sanatorium; Mr. Tadashige Fujimaru, my first friend in Japan; Hisako Okamura, for allowing me to see Nagashima with my own eyes; Doctor Yoriaki Kamiryo; my Yukuhashi Cosmate and Jono Cultural Center students; my Japanese in-laws; Yuki and

Sayon, for their love of reading; and my wife, Aya, and son, Sam.

In the United States: my family of women—my mother and sisters, Kim and Teresa; Grandma Talarigo for her stories; Uncle Dick for his letter; and my father, Grandpa Talarigo, and Grandma Carlos, so much of this book is you; Colum McCann, for his faith and friendship; my publisher, Nan Talese, and my wonderful editor, Lorna Owen, for her passion for this book and helping to make it better; and finally, to Karin, wherever you may be.

a note about the author

JEFF TALARIGO, a former journalist, lived in a Palestinian refugee camp where he wrote several works of short fiction that were published in literary journals, including *The Maryland Review, The Arkansas Review,* and *Chantch.* He has been writing and teaching English in Japan since the early 1990s, and lives with his wife and son on the island of Kyushu.

a note about the type

The text of this book is set in Perpetua, a typeface designed by Eric Gill and released by the Monotype Corporation between 1925 and 1932. This typeface has a clean look with beautiful classical capitals, making it an excellent choice for both text and display settings. Perpetua was named for the book in which it made its first appearance: *The Passion of Perpetua and Felicity.*